A Christmas Duet

A Christmas Duet

Washington Island Christmas
Book One

By
Annette M. Irby

Prism Effect
Publishing

A Christmas Duet

Washington Island Christmas: Book One

© 2020 Annette M. Irby

This story is a work of fiction and was entirely written by the author. All characters and events are the product of the author's imagination. Any situational similarities or resemblance to any person, living or dead, is coincidental or used fictitiously.

Scripture quotations marked (*NLT*) are taken from the *Holy Bible, New Living Translation*, copyright © 1996. Used by permission of Tyndale House Publishers, Inc., Wheaton, IL 60189 USA. All rights reserved.

Cover Design by Dineen Miller.

This book first appeared in the anthology *Melodies of Christmas Love*, published by Pacific Lights Publishing.

First print edition: Autumn, 2024
ISBN: 979-8-9853231-4-6

Published in the United States of America.

Also by Annette M. Irby

Stand-alone Novella

Love Letters

Novelettes

Husband Material

Her Nerdy Cowboy

Washington Island Romance

Finding Love in Friday Harbor, Washington

Finding Love on Bainbridge Island, Washington

Finding Love on Whidbey Island, Washington

Washington Island Christmas

A Christmas Duet

A Christmas Romance

A Christmas Gift

Dedication

Dedicated to my dear sister Karen. I'm so grateful to God for your friendship in my life and that we share Him in common. I have fond memories of walking beaches with you during your visits to this region. Hopefully, we can do that again someday. Until we see each other again, sending hugs. I love you.

"Give all your worries and cares
to God, for he cares
about you."

−1 Peter 5:7 NLT

One

The evening's chilled, salty wind brushed Kate Fleming's hair away from her face. Leaving her cello wedged under blankets inside her sporty station wagon, she locked the doors and headed toward the stairs. She'd rather cross Puget Sound on the Whidbey Island ferry's upper deck.

Lights from the terminal and other vehicles shimmered off the water as she found a spot on the main level. Salty air blew in whenever someone opened the outward doors. But here, inside, as people spilled into the space from the vehicle levels below, heat. Faint Christmas carols played overhead, and Kate tried not to flinch at how tinny the music sounded. Her best friend, Haley, accused her of being a music snob. So be it. Her compositions now garnered national attention. The Piano Guys had opened doors for instrumental musicians to find a larger audience.

Fellow passengers milled around, choosing their own nooks for the sail across Puget Sound to Clinton, Washington, from Mukilteo.

A passenger walked by with a paper cup piled high with whipped cream, and Kate caught a whiff of chocolate steam. Just what she needed. Her fingers were still frozen from waiting in her car for the second ferry to arrive. She'd turned off her engine like everyone around her, forgoing heat to protect waiting passengers from breathing car fumes.

She slipped from the vinyl bench seat and made her way to the concessions area. The café was one large square, near the center of the boat, with space to walk around and choose snacks or beverages. The aroma of popcorn and the odor of coffee were the strongest. But she found a banana muffin in the case and waited her turn to pump cocoa into a cup. Then, she squirted a dollop of whipped cream and joined the cashier line.

The scent of leather wafted off the man in

front of her. His sherpa-lined brown leather jacket shone in the ferry's interior lighting. He stood a few inches taller than herself, cell phone in hand and plastic, wireless earbuds jutting straight down about an inch from his ears. They were about five people back in line and Kate sipped her cocoa, knowing the risks of whipped topping decorating her nose. She reached for a napkin, glancing over at leather-jacket guy. His phone tilted, and she caught a glimpse of the screen.

The MP3 player application displayed an oh-so-familiar album cover—hers. Well, her ensemble's. Whoa, this guy who looked a bit like a lumberjack, with his jeans—and was that plaid flannel under his jacket?—listened to her music? Instrumental? She'd peg him for country or classic rock but not cello with piano. She tucked herself behind him in line again, unable to squelch a smile. She wanted to ask his opinion. Did he like the melodies she'd invented? Which instrument did he favor? Her ensemble included a guitarist, pianist, and a vocalist who rarely sang words. And of course her cello, the lead instrument on several tracks of their latest record.

Lumberjack Guy hummed a familiar

refrain, and she caught her breath. Plenty of background noise droned on the boat. But this guy's baritone voice carried easily. Clear and smooth. She could listen to him all evening. Was he a musician as well?

"Is that everything?" the cashier asked him.

The humming stopped. Perhaps he only wore one earbud. "Yes, thanks." He paid for his beverage, then it was her turn. She'd chickened out—not speaking to him. It'd be lame to follow him, pepper him with questions about his musical preferences, hound him for his opinions, right? He was probably walking back to his girlfriend or wife.

A few minutes later, Kate spotted him sitting alone on one of the long benches near the windows in the dining area. Maybe an employee commuting? An air of melancholy surrounded him. At times, he'd stare through the windows, wearing almost a haunted expression. Compassion swelled inside, along with the crazy urge to give him a hug.

She'd keep her distance. But she could pray. *Lord, please help him, whatever his needs are.* People all around her faced their own hardships, no doubt. He seemed burdened.

She parked herself with her cocoa and

muffin at an empty table where she could watch him across the salon. He didn't stare down or swipe his screen, but rather, sat back, closing his eyes, as if escaping in the music.

He jolted alert when a child ran by, screaming, tugging a toy behind him, his parent following. He sipped his beverage and glanced around. So many people milled about, sitting, standing, walking as the boat moved across the Sound. Surely he wouldn't peek in her direction. But he did, and she dropped her gaze. Her muffin tore apart easily, and it melted on her tongue—a sweet banana flavor with a few crunchy walnut pieces.

She snuck a glance in his direction once more. A group of military uniform-clad folks gathered near his bench, chatting with the soldier sitting across from her lumberjack fan. He stood up, waving for them to sit, smiling, possibly thanking them for their service. Fitting for today of all days—Veteran's Day. The naval base on Whidbey drew plenty of military personnel. Lumberjack Guy respectfully strode away, found a different seat.

Silly of her to consider what he thought, what he was doing. Especially now with her newly bare ring finger. She pulled out her phone, checking for texts as she finished her cocoa.

Are you nearly here, girl? Can't wait any longer. Haley's message had come through about thirty minutes ago. Oops.

Hey! Finally caught a ferry. Having cocoa onboard. Need real food soon.

Ah! Okay I got you girl. You will find fresh-ish lasagna for the first night of our girls' long weekend. Just get here already.

I'm tryin'!

Kate switched to her map app and typed in the address for Haley's family beach house. Map shows about 50 min. Keep the pan warm?

On it. We've got some chores to do this weekend. I mean, if you still want to decorate this early for the holidays.

The ship's engines cut back, slowing the ferry as it approached the dock on the Clinton side. You know I do. I've been listening to Christmas carols for weeks.

Oh, I don't doubt it.

At the dock. TTY soon.

Halfway down the stairs toward the vehicle deck, Lumberjack Guy held the door for her to walk through. She did, smiling at him. He wouldn't recognize her. The only way fans recognized group members was if they'd seen them in concert, knew them personally, or watched their handful of videos on YouTube. Or if they checked out their website.

"Thanks," she said as she passed through the doorway.

"Sure."

"Merry Christmas!"

He chuckled but didn't return the greeting as he jogged down the stairs behind her. Yeah, most people weren't too into letting Christmas usurp Thanksgiving. But Kate loved Christmastime. In her heart, the holiday season began in mid-October.

She got into her station wagon but didn't fire up the engine, since again, no one wanted to be trapped here on the ferry's deck, breathing everyone's exhaust while waiting for the workers to lower the metal ramp, remove the chain barriers, and wave them off onto dry land. Chilly wind whipped between the vehicles on this open-air level, and she anticipated blasting her car's heat as soon as possible.

Minutes passed while the staff, clad in reflective vests, worked on the dock. Soon, she'd flip on her Christmas music and hum her way to Haley's beach house. If only it weren't already so dark for this drive.

Zachary Tillmon climbed into his truck, waiting for his turn to flip the ignition and drive off the ferry. His seven-year-old son played at Zach's sister's house, and he needed to get to sleep at a good hour. School holiday today but not tomorrow.

Already running late, he'd missed the first boat and had to wait for the next. But his sister and brother-in-law would feed Topher, and his son would have fun with his cousins until Zach could get there. Zach dreaded the silent treatment his son had chosen lately. Trying to get him to talk about what bothered him didn't help. Topher would shut down even tighter.

The staff waved him off onto the island. What Zach *wouldn't* do was tell Toph why he'd gone off island today, or what the doctor had said. He wasn't even sure he'd tell his sister, and she could grill him like nobody else.

Drivers in the line of vehicles in front of him started their engines, and Zach followed them onto Whidbey. Darkness had fallen a couple hours ago, but it was only 6:30. Still, it'd take him almost an hour to get to his sister's on the north end of the island. He settled in for the inky drive.

Punching the power button for his truck's CD player, he cued up the second track. The cello led on this one. Oh, he loved the sound of that instrument. Maybe because his mother had played as he was growing up. Something about this melody—original from what he knew—touched him deeply. It seemed to reach into his soul and give him a sense of contentment. Well, if he could forget his worries, it would.

This week, he had to find a second job. His music director salary at his church wouldn't cover his upcoming medical bills. But he'd find something. Maybe holiday work.

The melody attempted to transport him from this gloomy highway to someplace... peaceful. He needed a dose of peace. *Lord, I could use Your help here.* Pride kept him from confessing what Jesus already knew—Zach was scared, for himself and for his son. He both wanted answers and didn't mind waiting the few weeks the doctor talked about.

A band of fog lay across the road in front of

Zach, and he flipped on his fog lights, slowing his truck. Testing the wet pavement with a brake tap to see it if was slippery. No trouble yet. Other ferry travelers were out here—he'd seen a few SUVs and cars taking the right from the dock onto Hwy 525. He kept a safe distance behind the guy in front of him. Too bad the car following him didn't do the same. Sure, with temps around forty-five degrees, there wouldn't be ice, but he may need to slam on his brakes to avoid a deer. Then the car behind him would wedge itself right under his truck bed. Was the driver crazy? Inexperienced? He tightened his grip on the steering wheel. He hated tailgaters.

He hated a lot of things about other drivers' decisions.

Two

Stupid fog. Kate clung to the truck's tail-gate. The pickup's driver seemed to know where he was going. Spotty service might take out her map app, and then what would she do? She sure couldn't see the turnoffs in this soup. Chances were this guy in front of her, whoever he was, was headed to Birch Harbor too. Of course, he could pull off at any point and she'd be left out here on her own, in the dark.

Don't think about it. But the mist seemed sinister and far too similar to that evening last spring.

The truck in front of her slowed and she slapped her brake pedal, her breaths coming in short gasps. The readout on her dash didn't mention any chance of ice, but you never knew. November could bring ice or snow to the temperate rainforest that was Western Washington.

She eased her foot off the pedal as the driver gained distance between them. Her phone's light kept up its soft glow from the dash-mounted holder, the map guiding her to Haley's. She'd hoped to avoid this—arriving after dark. *Driving* after dark. But in thirty-two minutes she'd be there.

That stretch of fog had lifted, and she allowed herself a deep breath. She'd be okay. She'd passed Freeland and was coming up on Greenbank when the truck ahead pulled off the road and left her without an escort. *Ugh.*

Strangling the steering wheel, she passed the pickup, which then pulled back onto the road behind her. Oh great. Now he'd blind her all the way into Birch Harbor with his raised headlights and fog lights.

"Our long-awaited girls' weekend—will. Be. Worth. It." Her audible pep talk did little to calm her trembling. Using her teeth, she yanked off her gloves and flung them into the passenger seat. Seeing spots, she adjusted the buttons for her rearview side mirrors so those blinding truck lights weren't such a threat to her already limited night vision.

Thirty is too young to die. Thirty is far too young to die. Plus, she had music to write for her band's next album come the new year. They counted on her. *Lord, help?*

The guy behind her flipped off one set of lights, so the threat was reduced by half now. Heaven help them if more fog snaked across the island ahead. This thin stretch of land wasn't so wide that any marine humidity couldn't sock them in from west to east in a moment's notice. She slowed, and the truck kept a respectable distance.

Perhaps the driver was trying to send a message: *This, you nut bar, is the correct distance for driving on a dark, foggy, island highway. Take. Note.*

She laughed at her own inner conversation and kept her eyes on the road. With little oncoming traffic, and no one in front of her, she had one advantage the guy behind her didn't—high beams. She used them liberally for the remaining miles. One more little jog up into the hills on the east side of the island and she'd be there, joining Haley for lasagna and girl talk.

Finally.

Maybe the other driver took the hint, but it didn't matter now that Zach followed them. He or she hadn't hit anything or swerved off the road, even without Zach in front of them, guiding them to Birch Harbor like Rudolph.

That certain intersection lay ahead. Habit—and probably fear, or worse, insecurity—urged him to turn off the highway. Avoid this route. Take a detour. But it'd been years. What were the odds anything bad would happen here, again? Either his therapy was effective, or it wasn't. *Lord, either You have me or You don't.* Which, of course, He did. But hadn't He also had Hannah?

Last chance as he passed the turnoff on his right.

Hold on. What was that driver do—?

The wagon swerved, slamming to a stop and though Zach had been far enough back not to tailgate, the roads were wet and he couldn't stop in time. His truck hit their car with a jarring crash, pushing the shorter vehicle into the ditch on the right-hand side. His pickup followed, back end still on the gravelly shoulder.

Motion finally ended with a loud sigh Zach heard but didn't recall choosing to make—as if his own sounds were foreign to him. He peered through the night's darkness and filtered headlights' illumination to read the street sign at the corner.

An image of Hannah flashed in his mind. Beautiful. Full of life.

The odor of burned rubber filled his cab. He flicked off his engine, deadening the intake fan.

The driver appeared from the wagon, brushing off his clothes, but able to stomp toward Zach's truck. Short guy, from the looks of it, and was that a purple coat? Okay, maybe he'd guessed wrong...

She made eye contact in the dimness, and he shook off his confused thoughts. Definitely not a guy. Parking her hands on her hips, she waited for him to appear outside.

If only Hannah had gotten up that day, marching with indignation toward the other driver.

He'd barely gotten his door unlatched when Purple Coat opened the valve barricading her

words. "Didn't you see that deer?"

No, he hadn't. "I'm sorry. Are you all right?" He gave her a once-over. Judging by the fire shooting from her eyes, she was unharmed.

"I saw you on the ferry." She blinked a few times as if trying to connect the dots. It wasn't so unusual for ferry passengers to travel the same route once leaving the boat. Shaking off what looked like distraction, she scuttled down the slope toward her car's hood. "I'm glad I didn't hit that deer. But I still have front-end damage from this stump."

"At least I was far enough behind you to avoid a serious accident." *Really? Pettiness?* He was better than that. Maybe he should opt for silence. But c'mon. Did she realize she'd been riding his tail for several miles before he'd let her pass him? And had he seen *her* on the ferry? Probably, but she hadn't left an impression.

"'Serious'? You don't call this"—she nodded toward the mangled mess—"serious?"

"You seem fine, are you? Did you break anything?" Had the at-fault driver from years ago gone through similar moments with Han— *Do not go there. Just don't.*

She eyed him as if he'd grown a third eye.

"My car is wrecked, and I swear to Pete—" She darted toward her car's crunched liftgate, yanked out her phone, and hit the Flashlight app. Peering into the back, she studied whatever precious cargo she carried. "Oh, it seems okay."

His blood went cold. "Is there a child in there?" He'd never forgive himself. Never.

"It's not a child. But it is my baby." She fiddled with her phone, blinding him momentarily. He scrunched his eyes closed. "Now, what's your name and your insurance company?" She took a photo of his mangled front bumper, flash on, probably capturing his license plate. More spots swam in his vision.

"I'll need your name and insurance info too." Great. Raised premiums. Just what he didn't need. But if she was okay, that was all that mattered.

"Now, I'll have to get my car repaired."

"Same."

If looks could harm, hers had him half-mutilated on the way to his death. "So sorry for the inconvenience." Sarcasm dripped from her words like the drizzle on this foggy night.

"I've already apologized. *You* could apologize for tailgating me halfway to Birch

Harbor." *Shut up, Zach.* Why was he egging her on? No question the driver from three years ago couldn't have done *that* with Hannah. Not when she was unresponsive.

"I am not the one who ran into you." Again, she gestured toward the crunched metal. "I hate foggy night driving," she murmured as if she was in shock and didn't realize he could hear her.

They exchanged names, and she took a photo of his insurance information. "My agent will be in touch. You'd better hope my baby isn't harmed. She's valuable."

C'mon. "What, do you have a prize-winning pygmy unicorn foal in there or something?"

She laughed, but it sounded irritated. "Know any tow truck drivers?"

He lasered in on her words like they were an assignment. "I do. I'll call him."

An hour later, while she rode shotgun, Carl hauled her munched station wagon down the highway toward Birch Harbor. Zach's truck would run. He'd follow in a few minutes. Give himself a chance to regain his bearings.

His sister was going to kill him for being so late. He'd have to cancel the get-together a friend had coerced him into. No way he had

the energy for auditioning a cellist tonight.
Next time he'd avoid this intersection.

Three

Kate waved off the tow truck driver as he left her and her vehicle at the beach house. *Finally.* She breathed a loud sigh in her empty vehicle, hands still shaking. But she'd made it.

What was with that other driver? First, he was Lumberjack Guy, wasn't he? She shouldn't have been so hard on him. "Pygmy unicorn foal?" She chuckled again in the quiet of her parked car. Well, since the guy–Zach, right?–enjoyed her ensemble's music, he couldn't be all bad. And he was kind to her at the scene.

He'd been correct. He hadn't ridden her bumper. But how had he missed the deer her high beams practically spotlighted? She may have a sore neck in the morning. Plus the headache of car repairs and insurance haggling. *Welcome to girls' weekend.*

Focus on the positives. She'd get to spend the next several weeks here. On the island. In a beach house! If that didn't inspire her, nothing could. *Help me, please, Lord. You have been so generous to me.*

She'd had the tow truck position her car next to this left-side entrance along the street side of the house. How had Haley not heard the hubbub of the truck delivering her and unhooking? Kate assumed she'd come running. Studying her vehicle's damage, she caught another whiff of salty air blowing in from Puget Sound on the night wind. Lights shimmered on the bay. Come tomorrow morning, she hoped to awake to the glorious view that waited out there. Maybe that could ease her stress. For now, she breathed deep. *I'm safe.*

Haley met her at the cute little gate beside the garage. "You're here!" She hugged her, and her long nearly black hair curled into Kate's face. "Let me help you with your bags." Motion sensor lights flipped back on, and Haley stopped at the rear liftgate and gasped. "What happened?"

"Crazy deer. The driver behind me couldn't stop in time." Irritation returned. He'd had the nerve to scold her for tailgating. *She* hadn't run into him. Birch Harbor wasn't a big city, but hopefully she'd avoid seeing him again this week.

"Are you all right?" Haley looked her over.

"I'm fine. Nothing your lasagna can't fix." She pushed the button to open the back, but nothing happened. "Uh-oh. How will I get my cello out?" She certainly couldn't leave it in the cold car overnight. "Any chance I can pull my car into the garage?"

"Absolutely. And I may know a guy who can get this open for you tonight."

"Oh, that would be great." If she'd thought about it, maybe that tow truck driver could've helped. She hadn't been able to lower her back seat for years. Maybe between the two of them, the women could heft the case over the headrests and pry it out through a side door.

"I know how much you worry about your baby. Let's get you sorted."

Kate settled behind the wheel and soon had her station wagon safely inside the protected garage. Twenty minutes later, Kate and Haley were winded from trying to free her cello.

She'd climbed into the back and verified. The case was undamaged. *Thank You, God.*

The back seat would not lower. Haley stepped away from the wagon, and Kate heard her on her phone while Kate tried to problem solve. Why hadn't she had these levers fixed when she could? She'd never assumed the lift-gate would cease working. The idea of an accident always wigged her out, knowing her expensive cargo.

Haley reappeared at the open passenger door. "I got ahold of my guy. He has to take care of something, but he'll be over after that. He couldn't really give me a timeline."

"Oh, I'm just glad he's willing to try. That's nice of him. I could have asked the tow truck driver earlier. But it's probably for the best since I still haven't taken pictures of the whole thing. You know how insurance adjusters are. They need to see the actual damage."

"Of course. Still can't believe I didn't hear the truck. I was vacuuming upstairs, trying to keep busy. My guy also said his mechanic friend–Carl?–can probably get in if he can't. Like pry the door open. You'd better go take those pics before he gets here."

Right now, her priority had to be her baby

over her transportation. If she had to, she could afford a new vehicle. She'd been debating for a while. But it had felt wasteful to replace a working car. So, she invested her resources in other areas—like renting this place for a season of writing.

Kate climbed back out and marched to the rear liftgate. She took pictures of the damage from as many angles as she could. The overhead light only helped so much, so she turned on her flash. "Do you want to go grab a space heater? That should warm the atmosphere until your buddy gets here."

"Done."

Zach pocketed his phone and climbed out of his truck. Haley hadn't said much, only that she needed his help with a car problem at her family's mansion. He'd head there in a bit.

Zach's sister, Lacy, kept a cozy home. As he walked in, the aromas of hot apple cider, cinnamon, and baked macaroni and cheese hit him in the stomach. Of course, he couldn't stay long. He needed to help Haley and her friend. But he wouldn't bail on his sister or his son either.

"Hey, big brother!" Lacy's house was a traditional northwest design with two stories, a split-level entry, and bedrooms over the garage. Her husband worked in contracting, so he spent free time remodeling this forty-year-old house they'd owned for six years.

"Hey, Sis." Zach hugged her, already certain he wouldn't bring up the accident. "Sorry about the delay. Where's Toph?" He'd get ahead of this conversation because knowing his sister, she planned to grill him about why he'd needed a sitter today.

"Playing with his cousins. I fed them an hour ago. They were *starving* from building forts all day."

"Of course they were."

Lacy's husband, Adam Flynn, stepped into the kitchen from the den. "Hey, Zach." They fist bumped. "How goes everything?"

"Fine." Adam was a good guy, but Zach was out of energy for small talk tonight.

Lacy ambled to the oven and pulled out a pan of baked cheesy goodness, which she set on a trivet. She slapped three huge spoonfuls of macaroni onto a plate. Pointing across the tiled bar, she motioned for Zach to sit. He dutifully obeyed. Lacy was tiny, but she was a force he didn't have the strength to fight. Plus, his stomach demanded food and his sister knew how to cook.

She handed him a bowl of steamed broccoli and another of dark, glistening grapes. He slathered butter onto a thick slice of crusty French bread. "You spoil me, Sis."

"Our pleasure," Lacy said. Adam joined her and gave her a side hug. "But something's eating you. So, while you inhale that, I'll grill you with questions. Mm-kay?"

Her husband snorted. "I'll go see what the kids are up to. They've been quiet too long." Facing Zach, he added, "Good luck."

Lacy occupied herself with kitchen cleanup while Zach wished for cello music.

"So, what's up? Is it Topher? Or the anniversary?"

She never did pull punches, his sister.

"Or maybe you're ready to tell me about your doctor's visit."

He gulped ice water and set his cup down too loudly on the hard-surface countertop. Realizing he could have shattered the glass, or cracked a tile, he shifted his drink to the place mat Lacy insisted the kids use. The muffled thud wasn't nearly as satisfying.

"I mean, did you think I wouldn't ask?" She propped a hip against the counter. "Spill it."

His sister was his closest confidante, and he trusted her. But he wouldn't be transparent this time. "I don't want to worry you."

"Too late." Arms crossed over her chest, she gave him the eagle eye she used on the kids.

"Doc removed the mole. Now, we wait."

"She was concerned enough to remove it and not simply monitor it?"

"Yes."

Last winter, when Zach had bronchitis, his local doc had found a suspicious mole on his chest. Worried about skin cancer, he'd referred Zach to a dermatologist in Mukilteo. "I guess she just wanted a piece of me."

"Har-har." Lacy's expression went sober. "I don't like this."

"Neither do I." He made eye contact. "Look. It may be nothing. She's just being careful. You know, avoiding lawsuits. It's not as if I, a music director at church—indoors—have come down with melanoma."

"We never did lie out in the sun, not while growing up here."

So many overcast days. "Right?" He

resumed eating, putting on the façade that all was well. For her. "Nothing to worry about." Except he needed to get his will in order, for Topher's sake. He reined in a loud sigh.

"Keep me updated?"

He'd rather not. If worse came up he'd need her to babysit though. And they'd already settled that she and Adam would raise Toph if anything happened to Zach. Just like Zach would take Lacy's kids if anything happened to her and Adam.

Doc said if the test came back suspicious, they'd need to take a bigger chunk out of him. But he'd keep that to himself for now. "Could be a few weeks."

"Fine. Now, about Toph . . ." Her words trailed off, but he knew where she was going.

He nodded. "I'm worried about him." Anxiety robbed Zach's appetite.

"He was too young to know it happened this month." She kept her voice down, like Zach had done. "I'm sure he doesn't understand."

"And yet, this is the time of year he gets so solemn. I thought last November and December would be the hardest. But no, here we are again."

"Something about the holidays, then." She

absently wiped at the stainless-steel sink's edge with a damp dishcloth. "So, it'll probably lift by January when he heads back to school after winter break."

"And until then?" He shoved his plate of food away, half-eaten.

"I know you never expected to do this alone." Lacy's voice cracked.

Sometimes he forgot how close she'd been to—

"Your dad's here, kiddo," Lacy called as a stampede charged into the room behind Zach. He cleared his throat and his expression.

"Pack up your things, buddy. Time to head out." Zach turned and watched his seven-year-old son obey without any enthusiasm or complaint. Yeah, the kid was on shutdown. There were plenty of reasons, if Topher was old enough to understand. Zach battled not to let this time of year get *him* down so much that he couldn't parent his son. And today's accident only grated on him. He shoved those thoughts aside.

Zach kept up a good front. Tried not to let his inner scowl show. Tried to make sure Topher had all he needed for school holiday celebrations.

Simply tried to get them through the season.

Four

"Hey, Zach and Topher," Haley said as soon as her mansion's garage door stopped grinding. "Please meet my BFF, Kate Fleming."

Couldn't be. Birch Harbor was too small today. Zach rubbed the back of his neck and held on to Topher's shoulder. Otherwise, he might run off.

"We've met," Kate said, freeing herself from the back passenger side. "He's the guy who ran into me."

"No way." Haley eyed them both, one after the other.

Zach would rather shield his son from this conversation. He rubbed his neck. "My apologies. Again."

Kate started to climb back in. What? Was she going to wrestle her cargo over the rear seats without lowering them? "Thanks for stopping by, but I think we can get my cello out this way. Have a good night," she called over her shoulder, sending him on his way.

Haley's chagrin showed in her expression, and she gestured for Topher to join her on the empty side of the garage. Then she closed the big door, which would keep what little heat that puny space heater pumped out in the cavernous garage. Why were they going to that much trouble? Were they cold? It wasn't *that* chilly tonight.

"It seems she's a little put out still," Haley said under her breath while the door lowered. She pointed toward the munched wagon Zach had hoped to never see again. "Still, we've tried everything."

"Stay with Miss Haley, okay, Topher?"

His son shrugged.

"I've got him," Haley promised, and Topher seemed comfortable. So Zach approached the opposite side of the wagon. The vehicle's interior lighting popped on, and he caught a glimpse of her precious baby. A cello. Ah. That explained their worry. Barring other options, his mother would have lit a fire in the center of the cement floor to keep her instrument from warping in this humidity and winter air.

Haley had wanted him to audition a cellist, but for some reason Zach assumed she was elderly. No way Haley had meant Kate. Too coincidental. He refocused on the issue. The rear liftgate was dented inward. The release wasn't working. But why didn't Kate choose the obvious solution?

"Let me." He reached for the lever to lower the seat on this side.

Kate eyed him. "Don't bother. Both sides are broken. I've been meaning to get them fixed."

"Both sides?" Hmm. With the headrests as high as they were, that presented a problem. Maybe they would have to open the back, somehow. He may still need to call Carl. Her cello should not stay out here overnight. "Mind if I look at that side?" he asked her.

She backed out and waved. "Be my guest."

He pulled the right-hand lever and still the seat wouldn't budge.

"We've tried everything. Thanks anyway." She really wanted to get rid of him. But he hadn't solved this yet.

"What if we take a headrest off? At least on this side?" He knelt on the seat, facing backward. But he wouldn't touch it until he had her okay. He might not be able to replace it once it came off. *If* it came off. How old was this wagon anyway? It seemed sporty enough to be newer, but with broken levers, he had to wonder. She'd probably bought it used, quirks and all. "All right with you?"

"That's a new idea." She leaned into the car, toward him. Her scent—something tropical—washed over him. Huh. Yum. "Think we can remove it?" she asked.

He refocused and reached toward the nearest headrest, giving it a tug. "Usually, there's a button to release it fully from the neck..." Sure enough, his fingers landed on the switch and the piece tugged off into his hands. "Voilà."

"You did it, Dad!" Topher said from across the room. Pride surged, just a hint, and Zach refocused.

"We'll need to watch this sharp metal piece now. I don't want to lower it too far because it may vanish and then I won't be able to get this back on."

"Fair enough."

Zach pressed himself against the split

bench seat and tugged the cello closer by its neck. Kate backed up. "I should be able to..." He lifted and pulled and soon had the cello case suspended, almost pressing the wagon's ceiling, before he could pass one end to Kate outside.

She received it, and he carefully shifted to lift the heavy end of the instrument toward her.

"We got it!" Kate called as she set the wide end of the case at her feet. She held the top and inspected the shell. "She looks good."

He stifled a sigh of relief. He'd have hated to be responsible for damaging someone else's prized instrument. She'd mentioned value. He didn't doubt it. Kate disappeared into the house. He worked to get the headrest back into place. Time to take his son home to bed. A few minutes later, he had everything set and all the doors closed. Haley went about turning off the space heater and chatting with Topher.

"Everything looks good," Zach told Haley.

She gave a head tip toward the house's entrance. "She's probably tired. We appreciate you coming over and solving this."

"No problem."

One press of the button and the large

garage door ground overhead, letting in fresh sea air once it was open. "So, one more question before you two guys take off."

Zach opened his truck's passenger door, and Topher climbed in. "Shoot."

"Remember how you brought up needing more performers for the church's Christmas program? And I mentioned my friend, the cellist?" With her playfulness, Haley reminded him of Lacy.

Wait, Kate *was* the cellist Haley wanted him to audition? The same woman he'd crashed into. Oh, no. After all this, he would never consider asking Haley's BFF to volunteer to perform. Not a chance.

He cleared his throat. "No worries. I think my slots are mostly full."

"I mean, we're still free tomorrow night if you wanted to come back." Haley gave him a pleading face, and he couldn't make himself squash it. He'd text her tomorrow to gently let her down.

"Let's wait and see." He strode to his side of the truck.

"Thanks again."

"'Night, Haley."

Yeah, around lunchtime the next day, he'd

cancel the audition plans. No matter how good Kate smelled.

Kate sat at the table, inhaling lasagna when Haley returned. Banging sounds rang down the hall as if Haley was storing the space heater once again in the hall closet.

She moved to the prep sink to wash up. "You could have come back out and thanked him. He did save your cello, after all."

"Ack, you're right, I should have." Zach Tillmon. Why did Haley have to be buddies with him? At least that was the last time she'd have to see him. The fact of the collision hadn't sunk in yet. Another car accident. No doubt she'd have flashbacks at bedtime. The upside? The crash wasn't her fault this time. "Tell me he's gone."

"He is." Haley peeked under the table. "I see you've already donned your fluffy polar bear slippers."

Kate wiggled her feet, letting herself relax for the first time in several hours. "You know it."

Standing at the closest island, Haley studied

Kate with all the discernment of a BFF. "Are you sure you're okay?"

"At the moment, yes." Not like last spring.

"I'm glad you're safe."

"Grab some hot tea. Join me," Kate suggested.

For a few minutes, Haley busied herself boiling water and opening cupboards. "Where's your baby?" she asked when she joined Kate at the table with a teacup, bringing the scent of apples and cinnamon with her.

"In the den." Kate had set the case on the floor and opened it to inspect her instrument. Not so much as a scratch. *Thank You, God.* If she had to, she could replace her cello, but she'd rather not. They'd shared too many miles, too many shows. Of course, replace was worst-case scenario. She'd start with a repair. Thankfully the impact of Zach's truck hadn't resulted in needing either.

"Good thinking. We can cart it to the living area with the piano whenever you like—you brought the stand, yes? But in there it'll be protected while we haul out the Christmas decorations this week."

Oh, Kate loved this house. The great room with its combination kitchen and living space and soaring ceilings. Haley's family had recently remodeled the home, updating every element—granite, stainless, marble, wood flooring, furniture. A balcony railing perched to the upper right when she faced the white baby grand piano. "This room is going to look gorgeous with holiday decorations set up."

"It's a good thing I'm willing to tolerate your quirks, girl."

Kate pointed toward the gorgeous, well-lit kitchen with its two islands, breakfast bar, eat-in dining area, black countertops, and gleaming appliances. "I'm so grateful to your parents for letting me rent this house on the friends-and-family discount."

"They're happy to help. And I'll like having you nearby."

"Feel free to sleep over whenever you want, though I know you like your apartment better."

Haley made an elegant gesture, pinky out, teacup raised. "I want to give you room to create."

Kate adopted the same snobby tone of voice. "And I appreciate it, *dahling.*" She returned to her normal voice. "It solved my sudden housing issue. I couldn't very well stay with the honeymooners." Before her cousin and roommate married recently, Kate had found other housing. But her subsequent roommate had just changed her mind.

"You're helping my parents out too. Now they don't have to worry about finding renters through the holidays."

Kate finished her meal. "I'm looking forward to this time with my BFF. No more run-ins with local guy friends, and I'm golden for the weekend."

Haley hopped up, grabbed Kate's plate, and headed to the far sink.

"Hales?" Kate said to her back as Haley yanked open the dishwasher and flicked on the faucet.

No answer.

Kate followed her and flipped off the hot water stream before taking the plate Haley held and standing it in the lower rack. Then, she faced her again. "Promise me we won't have to see Zach again this weekend."

"No can do, my friend."

"Why not?"

"Have I mentioned the music director at my church is doing a Christmas program? He's looking for performers. And since you'll be here for Christmas..."

A sinking feeling settled inside, given Haley's expression. Kate toyed with a dish towel, nerves rising. "That's not a threat, unless Zach wants me to perform *with* him. I'm guessing he plays an instrument. He and I could certainly be in the same program together, performing separately. No problem."

"He plays piano. And I assume he'll play for the program. After all, he's the music director."

"Zach is?"

"Yup."

"So, if I volunteer, I'll work with him on scheduling, song selection, rehearsal times, etcetera?"

"Yup."

Well, that was easy. "Okay, I just won't volunteer."

Haley quirked her lips and tightened her eyes. "Really? You'd withhold your gift of playing at Christmas?"

"Ack! Guilt trip."

"You already owe him a thanks for helping you out."

"No, I owe him a call from my insurance company. Which *will* be happening.

Tomorrow morning. Thank you."

Haley's expression said she'd tolerated enough arguments for the night, and she wouldn't allow this one. "You should reconsider. The guy needs help, or he may. He wasn't sure when I just asked him outside."

"What did you ask him?"

"If he still wanted to come over tomorrow and play for a while. With you. You know, hear you play."

Kate sputtered. She didn't mind auditioning, if *she* arranged it.

Haley held up her hands. "I mean I never meant to put you on the spot, of course." Her nose twitched—a telltale sign that Haley was in deep sheep here. "How was I to know he'd literally crash into you?"

Best to cancel now. Surely Zach would agree to call it off. In fact, he may already have planned to. "I think, considering all that's happen—"

"But it'd be rude to cancel now." Was Haley even listening?

"What if he's unwilling to come back? I mean, I've been really dismissive to him." Conviction chipped away at her confidence again. *Sorry, Lord. I'll make it right as soon as*

I can.

"He wouldn't stay long. His kid has school Friday. I didn't tell him about your fame, so it doesn't have to get weird."

"Ha. Fame. No one knows who I am by name." And most people probably didn't know her attachment to her ensemble. Theirs was a niche audience, though they gained popularity by the day.

"Well, you can decide if you tell him or not."

"Nice of you to give me that choice." It wasn't just the drive or her housing worries or the accident. Haley had no idea of Kate's other news. But maybe it could wait until breakfast.

Haley zeroed in on her with *that look*. "What's wrong?"

Maybe unburdening herself would help. "It shouldn't bug me as much as it does. I saw it coming for a while. And actually, I'm kind of relieved—"

"Out with it."

"Heath."

Haley leaned toward her over the table. "Uh-oh. What happened?"

Her list of reasons aside, Kate's heart stung.

Shaking her head, Haley continued. "I knew something was wrong at Amanda's wedding.

He didn't even sit by you at the reception. He was off chatting with—what was her name? Brenda?"

"Another cousin."

"Figures." Haley reached for Kate's free hand.

"You know what, though? I'd like to switch gears and watch Hallmark and drink cocoa. Sound good?"

"Done." Haley worked on hot chocolate prep while Kate found a Christmas movie and cued it up.

Rather than bring them closer together, her cousin Amanda's wedding had seemed to seal Heath's decision *away* from matrimony.

And *that* didn't hurt at all.

Kate shook off the slime of rejection. She needed a peaceful holiday season. In this glorious house, writing for her ensemble's next album. Nothing extra. Time to heal and press into God for inspiration.

And some feel-good movies with her BFF were a good way to begin.

Five

Zach had almost canceled tonight's plan. He would have if Haley hadn't been so convincing. She reassured him that the two women wanted Zach's and Topher's company. That Zach really *needed* to hear Kate play. He wouldn't believe how good she was, etc. And his Christmas program was sparse, despite what he'd said the night before.

He and Toph parked in the mansion's driveway, and he flipped off his headlights. Drizzle sparkled on the windshield, illuminated by the house's exterior lights.

Mid-afternoon, he'd heard from his insurance company and Kate's. An unwelcome ingredient added to his life this fall. But he wouldn't whine. He'd face his mistakes and find a way to fix the damage. Would Kate forgive him? Had she already?

Why was he here again?

Topher hadn't said a word since school let out. At times he could seem so animated, and others? He receded. Like tonight. "Let's go, buddy." He climbed out and went to his son's side of the truck where he opened the door. "This will be fun. You like Haley's house, right?"

Toph shrugged his shoulders. Zach stifled a sigh as they moved to the mansion's front entrance. Glass panels made up the door and the two flanking windows, and he caught a glimpse of opulence inside, lit by an overhead chandelier. Yeah, Haley Reese's family was loaded.

"Don't break anything, Toph, okay?"

Topher stayed quiet, that sullen demeanor firmly in place. Maybe Haley could entertain him with a craft. All Zach wanted to do was follow through with a quick visit, hear Kate play, politely acknowledge how good she was, no matter how she sounded, and take off.

Cello music. The reason he'd given in and agreed to come over. He hadn't played a piano-cello duet for at least three years. He should keep an open mind. Because if Kate was good, the Christmas program would benefit from her involvement. *If* she even considered it.

Haley appeared behind the glass window. She wore an orange sweater over skinny jeans, her almost-black hair in what his sister would call a messy bun. On Haley the style looked sophisticated, especially in this setting. But given her similarity to Lacy, he had zero attraction.

Not that he was looking.

Haley swung open the door. "Hi, guys. C'mon in!"

The noise of dishes clattering around the corner rang through the high-ceilinged house. Kate must be busy over there.

"You two mind leaving your shoes here by the door?"

He kicked his off, and his son obeyed as well. Then they padded behind Haley farther into the house, the hardwoods gleaming and somewhat slippery under foot.

"Hey, Topher. I have a surprise for you tonight, if it's okay with your father." She rubbed her stomach as if sending Zach a message involving sweets and sought his nod, then refocused on Topher. "I thought that while he plays music with Miss Kate, you and I could decorate cookies. Okay with you, Dad?" She grinned at Topher, but he stared at the floor.

"Of course. Sounds fun, buddy."

They stepped into the great room, and Zach's breath evaporated. He'd never been in here before. Wow. He imagined a stunning Puget Sound view during the daytime. A glistening white baby grand stood near a gas fireplace to his right, with seating of white sofas and chairs lining the room. Directly ahead, French doors led to a deck no doubt. And to the left, a huge black-and-white kitchen boasted a round table near the window.

Kate stood in the kitchen. He did a double-take. Had she looked this beautiful last night? Long brown hair glinted with a bit of gold from the overhead lighting. She glanced up from the sink and gave him a half smile, making dimples appear. He hadn't noticed those before either. The blue sweater brought out her eyes, another feature he hadn't appreciated until now. Of course, last night, those eyes were shooting flames at him for crashing into her.

"Hi again."

"Hey," he offered quietly. "Listen, if this is too weird, I'll totally understand."

She approached from the island, tossing a kitchen towel behind her. The fluffy white slippers on her feet caught him off guard, and he grinned. "I wanted to thank you for helping us with the cello."

"You're welcome."

"Now, okay with you if we leave all that accident stuff with the insurance companies?"

"Absolutely." He glanced toward the piano where her cello sat in its stand. "Is she okay?"

Kate must have known what he referred to, because she nodded. "Yes. She's fine."

Haley had already parked Toph on a barstool at the second island. She'd set out frosting and food coloring, plus two kinds of cookies in different shades—sugar and gingerbread?

Kate moved closer to them and stood on the opposite side of the bar. "I can't wait to taste what you two come up with. I'm glad you're here, Topher."

For her, he smiled. Yeah, Zach would too.

Zach stood with his hands in his pockets, though the gleaming piano called. "Thanks for hosting us tonight."

Haley handed Topher a plate. "Our pleasure. I hope this is helpful."

"Shall we?" Kate asked Zach as she pointed toward the instruments.

Since Haley had worked magic with his son, Zach followed Kate to the living area. He seated himself on the piano bench with his back facing the kitchen. Kate settled in a chair without arms, so her elbows were free. She seemed at ease, relaxed, and beautiful. He'd met plenty of women since Topher's mother but couldn't recall reacting to any of them like he was tonight—mesmerized, unable to focus, juvenile. *Get it together, dude.*

Bow poised, she gave him direct eye contact this time, like she'd done with his son. She wasn't lacking in confidence, but he didn't read pride either. Just a sense that she knew her instrument and wasn't intimidated. Did she play by ear too?

"So, what did you have in mind?" she asked him. Did she know this was an audition? If so, it didn't affect her approach.

"How about a Christmas carol?"

"Did you want me to play alone, or were you going to join in?"

It would be fun to play together. He'd be

able to tell if she was skilled enough for a solo at the program. "Together, if that's cool with you." He positioned his fingers over the familiar keys—not that he'd played on a baby grand often lately. This was an exquisite instrument.

She adjusted the pitch of one of her strings, tuning by ear. "Let's try 'Good King Wenceslas.'"

"Key of?" His fingers glanced over the ivories as he warmed up with a few scales. They settled on the key of A, and he played an intro into the song, keeping his expectations low.

She jumped right in with competence. Did she lead a group of musicians somewhere? That would fit given her instrument's rich tone and high value. Maybe she played with a regional symphony.

While she carried the melody, he filled in the embellishments. She kept up, every now and then glancing in his direction. Oftentimes she closed her eyes, ears attuned, like he often did. Her deft fingers slipped over the strings with ease. She played with emotion and in this lighting, her long hair seemed to glow.

Caught up in the way they were locked into the song together, he barely noticed when Toph came and stood next to Kate. Would he interrupt them? Zach wanted to shake his head in a gentle warning, but he needed to stay alert to keep up. Either she'd been doing this for a long time, or this was the one song she knew like her own name. Didn't matter; he liked what they created together.

She gave him a nod, and they ended the song after one final measure. He found himself grinning ear to ear, like a dork. He hadn't experienced that high—well, ever. Haley clapped. Kate beamed.

Zach glanced at his son. Surely, if anything could bring him out of his doldrums, it'd be music like that. *Lord, please help me out here with Toph. How can I ease his pain? I don't even know what's causing it.* A deep sadness filled Topher's face. Wha—?

After setting her instrument on its stand, Kate was right there, bending to make eye contact. "Topher, what happened? Are you in pain?"

Did he have an ear infection? Had they played too loud? Maybe his tummy ached from eating too much sugar. Lately, Zach felt they'd gone back in time to when Toph was a baby and he'd been unable to tell Zach what was wrong, always keeping him guessing.

Help, Zach prayed again as he crouched to eye level. Topher turned his back to him, but he didn't shrug off Kate's attention. Shoot. It sure would help if his son would let him get near, give him a chance to fix whatever was wrong.

Haley watched the interactions, exchanging worried expressions with Kate.

Zach straightened his back. "I think it's time I took him home. He's tired." Not that a good night's sleep would fix this, but these women didn't need to know that.

As Topher scrubbed a tear from his face, Haley guided him back to the island. "Let's wrap up your cookies, okay? You can take them home."

"Thanks."

All summer, he and Topher had played at the beach, kayaking in a two-person craft, building sand castles, skipping rocks, finding shells and crabs. Topher seemed like a happy kid. Then, bam! November rolled around, and he turned sad and clammed up.

Kate clasped her hands together in front of her chest, her expression uneasy. Had she noticed Topher wouldn't even look at Zach?

"Let's get our coats and shoes back on,

bud," he said, accepting the plate of cookies from Haley and guiding his son toward the front door. They'd gotten three frosted. Zach would be sure one of them ended up in Topher's lunch tomorrow at school.

"Thanks for visiting," Haley said, leaning toward Topher. "I hope you guys come back."

"Can we, Dad? Soon?"

He wanted to return? After his meltdown? Zach didn't feel right about imposing. Without committing, he slid his shoes on and then helped his son into his coat.

"That would give us a chance to play more music," Kate offered with an earnest tone. "I'm in. And, we'll have some Christmas decorations up." She exchanged glances with Haley. "Say, maybe, Saturday?"

Topher gave her a smile, and Zach's gut tightened. He'd missed that expression this fall. Toph glanced up at him. "Can we?"

He'd give his son the world to see him smile again. "If it's okay with Miss Haley and Miss Kate, then absolutely." Zach studied the women's faces.

"We're on!" Haley bent again and retied Topher's shoe. "I'll even make you guys dinner. What do you like to eat, young man?"

"Um . . . pizza!"

Haley peered up at Zach. *Okay with you?* she mouthed, and he nodded. "Homemade pizza it is."

These two women may be angels for how kindly they treated two guys trying to navigate the holidays without Topher's mom.

"See you both soon." Haley held the door.

Topher darted to the truck, and Zach turned to Haley. "Thank you." He included Kate standing there in her polar bear slippers. "Both of you. It was fun playing together."

Kate's smile shone in the porch lighting. "My pleasure."

They really had been able to set aside their first introduction, and the insurance haggling, to find common ground in music.

Kate leaned toward him. "Hey, one last thing. I wanted to apologize for tailgating you." She kept her voice down, maybe due to embarrassment.

"I thought we were leaving that aside. But thank you. I appreciate it."

She hugged herself. "Sorry about that, and my bad attitude . . . It's no excuse, but I have a hard time seeing at night, especially in fog." She gave a shiver as if she were suddenly insecure.

Well, that clarified that. Something protective rose inside, and he had a strange urge to hold her and ease any lingering fears or awkwardness. *Where did* that *come from?* "Gotcha. No problem." Never occurred to him that she may have wanted an escort. He should have stayed in front of her and "held her hand" all the way to Birch Harbor. "'Night."

"'Night." The women called in unison as Zach made for the driver's side. Against his better judgment, he was already looking forward to Saturday night.

Six

The following morning dawned bright, with sunshine pouring in the floor-to-ceiling banks of windows, glittering off the bay. Kate squinted at the onslaught as she padded into the kitchen where Haley worked on breakfast. "'Morning."

Haley flipped off the gas stovetop burner and brought a saucepan to the nearest island. "So, you gonna tell him who you are? That you're, I don't know, a famous cellist in the hottest, growing-more-renown-every-day instrumental ensemble around?"

"That was a mouthful, girl." She found a juice glass and filled it with OJ. "Let me have my breakfast before you grill me on the gorgeous guest from last night."

Her BFF did *not* need to know she'd dreamt of Zach's soft hazel eyes. His dark hair had a hint of red. During his visit, his jaw had been sprinkled with light brown scruff. He didn't strike her as particularly macho—rather he'd seemed almost bookish, yet strong. His was a quiet, unassuming way of navigating awkward social situations. And he had a sort of haunted look that touched a tender part of her heart. Like he'd lost someone or faced something hard.

She filled a small bowl with Haley's home-made oatmeal and topped the hot cereal with fresh, mixed berries set out for breakfast.

"Eat hearty. We get to tote Christmas decorations down from the attic this morning." Haley pointed her spoon at Kate. "'Gorgeous,' huh?"

"He wrecked my wagon."

"Hahaha! Welp. Yes he did."

Kate guffawed too, officially awake. "Okay, that sounded funny. I meant he crashed into my car."

"But he's an excellent pianist."

Kate pursed her lips and then sighed. "True." She took a seat at the table, facing the bay's sparkling blue water. "The insurance adjuster is coming today to take photos.”

"No problem." Haley brought her own bowl of cereal over and settled across from Kate.

How much of a hassle would this car repair cause? "It could take a while to hear about an estimate and then longer to complete the repairs."

"Good thing you were planning to stay on island for a while then."

They ate in silence for a few minutes. "Hey, what's up with Topher? He seemed brokenhearted." Sort of like his dad, at times. "What happened?"

"I think it's his mom. I don't know the story, but I'm sure you noticed they didn't bring anyone with them."

Kate swallowed her bite of sweet strawberry. "Right. I wondered about that, especially since there's a tan line on Zach's ring finger."

"You noticed his ring finger?" Haley's giggle echoed off the high ceiling. Great acoustics in here, which Kate had noted last night. Playing the carol with Zach—riding that high. She'd forgotten how intoxicating connecting in music could be when there wasn't underlying tension.

Kate shrugged. What could she say to that? Of course she wouldn't consider a romance right now following Heath's rejection. "Curiosity. That's it." Still, connecting with someone musically–there wasn't anything like it.

"You are wearing the dopiest grin." Haley spooned up more cereal.

Kate cleared away her smile. "What? Uh, nope. No more dating piano players." Never again.

"Reminds me–you haven't told me what happened, though I have a good guess. Heath?"

Kate took a break from shoveling warm oatmeal into her mouth and letting the blueberries burst on her tongue. The time had come to fess up. "He broke things off, on the ride back from the wedding."

"He didn't." Haley shook her head. "I never did trust that guy."

"Oh, c'mon. You were the one piling bridal magazines on me and telling me to dream of big weddings and beachy honeymoons. For a year."

"Right. At first. But, hon, twelve months follows the proposal and he still doesn't want to set a date?" She pointed her empty spoon in Kate's direction. "Uh-uh. I do not trust that."

"I need cocoa." Kate made for the far counter where the electric tea kettle waited. She'd known telling Haley about her breakup would sting. Haley gave her space momentarily, while Kate prepped a mug of hot chocolate. Just as she'd hoped, the fridge held a canister of whipped cream. She squirted it liberally into a mound of happiness to rival the rejection.

Haley cleaned up her own breakfast dishes, made herself some hot tea, and resettled at the table, waiting for Kate to return. "I'm on your side, you know."

"I know. It's just, I'm not sure how I feel."

Haley squinted at her, whether from sunlight or confusion, Kate could only guess. "Explain, please."

"You'd think after three years together, I'd be—I don't know. Devastated? But I'm not. I'm . . . oh, Haley, this makes me a bad person, I just know it. I'm relieved."

"You should listen to that and stop feeling ashamed. Why were you sticking it out with him? I mean, when it became clear he wasn't going to set a date anytime this decade?"

"Well, it's a new decade now, so does it matter?" She shrugged.

Haley reached for her forearm, apparently not falling for the false bravado. "Of course it matters, hon. Your heart, your future, your plans matter."

"Except, I know I can't settle down in one place right now. Our touring schedule fills most of the year. I'm in the studio other times, with Heath. He's just as nomadic as I am. Maybe it was wise to go slow, put off setting a date."

"Did it feel wise?" Haley could always read her.

"Nope. It felt like rejection." She stared at a motor boat cutting a white path in the bay.

"Which is probably the confusing part—relief plus rejection equals a resounding sting." Had Haley hidden a remarkably similar breakup in her own life? She deeply got this.

"Yeah, but you knew we weren't meant for each other." While Kate preferred to overlook the yellow flags in their relationship. "How?"

"I can tell when you're unhappy. And for about six months, you've been rather unhappy. Whenever Heath came up in conversation, your face clouded over."

"Any connection to why you invited the music director here?"

One of Haley's shoulders nudged up and down. "Unsure. Instinct maybe."

"We don't even know his marital status. I mean, did his wife leave? Is she on a trip somewhere? What's happening?" She gulped more cocoa, glad it had cooled a bit. "How well do you know him?"

"He and I attend the same adult Sunday school class. He reminds me of a big brother. I met Topher because I've taught the children a few times. Poor kid. Something happened this fall because he's usually more even keel. Not lately."

"His dad seems unable to get through to him. Did you see the way Topher turned his back on him? Ouch."

"Right. Maybe I could get him to open up about what's bothering him."

"Since you have some history with him, I think you should try."

"Good plan." Haley stood and carried her teacup to the sink for a rinse before placing it in the dishwasher.

One thing about having a great room with a fully visible kitchen—the counter and sinks had to remain clear or the whole aesthetic would suffer. Kate preferred closed off rooms, but this mansion was glorious and she felt pampered just being here. *Thank You, Lord.*

Haley dried her hands on a towel. "Ready to haul some boxes?"

"Let's do it." Since this used to be Haley's home, Kate was happy to let her take the lead on decorations. "Are we doing the tree today?"

"Let's begin with room décor, like hanging garland and decorating the windows and balcony railing. Maybe the mantel. Still considering whether we should decorate the piano. We could save the *trees* for tomorrow." She held up three fingers to indicate the number of artificial conifers they'd be decorating.

"The more the better. The piano's glossy white finish will reflect any lights we hang, so we may not need to put anything on top, except perhaps a light-weight centerpiece on a cloth." She cleared and rinsed her dishes. Then she clapped her hands together in excitement. "So glad you're humoring me."

Haley hooked her elbow and led the way to the staircase. "You mean about extending the Christmas season? I'm all for it."

They spent a couple of hours bringing

boxes into the room, planning, and redecorating. Haley's family preferred to keep things simple, elegant, thus the white furniture. They preferred clear lights and pine garland. The friends exchanged sky-blue sofa pillows with red and placed figurines of Mary, Joseph, and Baby Jesus on the mantel.

Sleeves rolled up, Haley stepped back, her ribbon of black hair in a ponytail. "The room's coming together. Shall we wait to hang stockings?"

"Yes." Kate surveyed the room. "Where are we putting the first tree?"

"I think this is the best spot." She pointed toward a space where an outlet occupied the gray wall below the bank of windows. "The second one will go there." Haley pointed under the balcony to a spot where the wall curved around toward the front door. "And one up in the family room."

They worked well together, breaking for lunch. Getting all her relationship confessions out helped Kate relax, but she was still worried about something.

How would she ever work with Heath again?

Zach pulled into the parking lot for the Garrison family nursery. He chose a spot near the edge where a Pacific madrone tree hung its peeling branches over his truck. Golden light hit it, highlighting the smooth, bare green trunk under the red-orange bark. Behind the barn, neat rows of various firs lined up for Christmas, filling his cab with a fresh, pine scent.

He'd known Clay Garrison for a while now, having met him shortly after moving here last spring. Clay had mentioned that if Zach ever needed additional work, he could use him in landscaping. Growing season was behind them, though folks may still hire yard crews since the ground rarely froze here. Given the rainforest climate, cleanup was always needed to clear away blankets of pine needles. With Thanksgiving two weeks away, Zach hoped for seasonal work with those trees—delivering or working the farm.

Clay stepped out of the barn and approached Zach. They shook hands. "Hey."

He was relieved Clay didn't mention his

dented truck. His insurance would cover the repairs, once he could work up the deductible. Since his vehicle was larger than the wagon, he hadn't sustained as much damage as her car. "How's it going?"

"Good, man. Your son at school?" Clay was a little taller, strong from all his landscaping work.

"Yeah, till three. I didn't know if you'd be here since you're only at the farm part time."

"Right. But we're gearing up for the holiday season, so I came by to help my dad." Clay had a kind demeanor, as if life had sanded off his rougher edges. Zach could relate. Topher hit it off with him when they'd met at church. And Clay's girlfriend, Liberty Winfield, was a compassionate, artistic soul. She appeared through the barn door, carrying an armload of pine wreaths.

"Hey, how's it going?" She waved as she joined them.

Zach tucked his chilled fingers into his leather jacket. "Good to see you. Looks like you've been busy."

Her red hair fanned in the wind. "Always working with plants."

"And art," Clay added, pride in his eyes as

he gazed at her.

"I'm going to run these to the shop. See you at church, Zach."

"Take care."

Zach returned to his reason for dropping by. "About the holidays, I wondered if you needed any help. I'm good with a saw and I can carry trees, assist in the greenhouse, operate a tractor, whatever you need."

"I'm glad you decided to take me up on my offer. Ever worked at a nursery before?"

"As a teen, but it's been a while. Quick study, though."

"I don't doubt it. And we can use you, but I'm afraid we may not have a lot of hours right away. At least not until the end of November, unless a big landscaping client chooses us. You know, schools, industrial complexes, that sort of thing."

"Anything you have will work, so long as I can get a heads-up. I need to schedule around Topher's school day and my church hours."

"Done." They shook hands again.

"Thanks, Clay."

"Sure thing. I'll call you. It'll probably be mostly weeknights and Saturday hours."

"Ok. And I need Sundays off." Zach spent

entire Sundays at the church.

"You got it."

Zach drove away knowing he'd have to get ahold of his sister and see if she wouldn't mind babysitting more often. But he'd landed his second job. Now he should be able to cover his upcoming bills.

Moving here last May had been a risk. His sister was local, and her large church needed a musical director. Plus, Zach had wanted to get his son and himself out of that house in Issaquah. Even though the accident happened on Whidbey, their house down south held too many memories. He hated to impose on Lacy for his new work hours, but since he'd mentioned his medical appointments, at least he didn't have to hide that from her. She'd understand.

Maybe, instead of calling Lacy, he'd drop by. It'd been a while since he'd checked with her on how she was doing with their parents' passing. Did she feel like he did, that you never got to hang on to the ones who mattered? That was his destiny and why he wouldn't date again. The ones he loved—and please, God, let nothing happen to his son, or his sister or her family—were *always* taken from him.

Was it true in reverse too?
Please, Lord, don't take me from my son.

Seven

I f that phone rings one more time, you *have* to answer."

"Not if it's Heath, I don't." Seriously? He couldn't respect her request for space? He had to keep pushing. Prism Effect was on a break after working constantly for ten months. Her requests for a week or two without his texts and phone calls proved ineffective. The challenges of dating someone in her ensemble. No separation between work and her personal life. She should have known better.

Kate and Haley labored together on the second-floor railing, stringing clear lights over and through the pine garland they'd wound in the last half hour.

Haley wore her scolding face. "Have you

talked to him since the breakup?"

"Nah." She would, she just hadn't yet. "I don't think it's too much to ask for a breather."

"He may be calling for the band's sake. How will you know if you don't talk to him?"

For that matter, he'd probably sent her a slew of texts. A stubborn place inside debated blocking him. Her professional persona won out.

"It's the what-ifs, Hales. What if he wants out of Prism Effect? What if he wants *me* out? What if he wants me back in his personal life?"

Hands empty, Haley straightened, stretching her spine. "So what if he does? Do you want *him* back?"

Her head wagged side to side. "Absolutely not."

"Are you angry at him, or is this an ego thing?"

Kate blew out a long breath, gaze toward the bay view over the balcony's railing. Filtered sunlight glistened off the frothy blue-gray water, highlighting the shipping traffic. "Both?"

Her cell phone rang again from her back

pocket, and she reached for it while holding up a hand to her BFF. "Fine." She clicked AN-SWER and spoke into her phone, striding to her room. "Hi, Heath. What's up?" Shoot, her voice sounded off. But whatever. She had to stop caring what he might think.

"We need to schedule studio time in January, I mean, if you want to stay in the group after everything. And I thought we could split composing so you do seven and I'll do seven and we'll meet two weeks early to learn them, add parts, etcetera." His words came out rushed, his phrases bleeding into each other. He sounded nervous, which wasn't like him. But he also sounded bossy, which *was* con-sistent. She'd always overlooked this side of him in the past because it was usually short-lived. Right now? It grated.

Kate closed her bedroom door and moved toward the glass slider overlooking the harbor. The deck on the other side called to her, but given the noisy wind, she'd stay put. She'd keep her tone calm and stay reasonable, even if he pushed her buttons. None of what he'd said was news though. She waited for him to continue with new information.

"What, did you think I'd flake?" he asked.

And now, he sounded defensive. Super.

She scoffed. "You mean like you did with our wedding plans?"

"What plans? We never made any."

"Exactly." She clenched her fist and then unclenched it at her side. "Forget it. I'm fine with composing. I've always done the bulk of the writing. I'll probably bring closer to ten, and the group can narrow them down. Now, about setting a rehearsal date. One sec." She pushed the SPEAKER button on her phone and pulled up her calendar app. "Let's meet the seventh of January in Gig Harbor at Beth's. We'll go over everything and narrow down the song choices. Set studio time for two weeks later." Beth, their vocalist, usually hosted them for writing sessions.

"I'll call Jon and set it up." Heath referred to their producer. "By the way, I don't see myself as 'flaking' on our engagement." And here came his condescending tone—her least favorite. "I mean, even *you* would have to admit—"

She clicked DISCONNECT and repocketed her phone. No, she didn't have to admit anything. Not to him. Maybe to Haley. She sure didn't need to listen to him mansplain anything to her.

Either way—she had dodged a missile not marrying him, the jerk.

While they dated, she consistently overlooked the myriad ways he irritated her. He happily let her carry the biggest burden for their group—compose the most, labor the hardest. She didn't mind contributing, but at times even the other members mentioned how he took advantage of people, micromanaged everyone, and weaseled out of his commitments.

Like their engagement.

How would they work together again? Previously, they'd collaborated with their music—each bringing a strength. The group relied on Kate and Heath to come up with original music. Now? She not only didn't want to see him or talk to him again, she definitely never wanted to tour with him again. Close proximity without escape. Trying to find their way musically without fighting. The whole thing made her feel slightly ill. What had she ever seen in him? And worse: Why had she stayed with him so long?

Those questions kept her up at night. At first Heath had been kind, warm, romantic. His piano playing sparked her imagination.

They sounded great together, easily read each other. Could they get that back?

She stepped onto the deck off her room into the brisk, late-afternoon air. Prism Effect was her life, her future. Her identity. And they were finally seeing success. All her hard work was paying off. She couldn't walk away from that now. Not when she'd been the one to start, and then subsequently carry, the ensemble.

What was she going to do?

She made her way back to the indoor balcony overlooking the living area. Haley fiddled with minor adjustments to the winding garland as if waiting for her to reappear. "So, how'd it go?"

"You mean before or after the mansplaining attempt?"

"Gag. He didn't."

"Oh, he did."

"One more part of his personality that always grated on me."

They stacked the empty totes for a later trip to the attic, and then went down the staircase to eye their work. Kate peered at her best friend. "Why didn't you ever tell me your concerns? I would have listened."

"Nah. I figured you'd see what you needed

to in time. And thankfully, you did."

"If only I'd been strong enough to call it." The truth still stung—that *he'd* broken it off, not her.

"That's what's bothering you—he broke up with you."

"Mind reader. I'm a terrible judge of character, obviously." She straightened her spine. "So I've made a few decisions. The key is to one, avoid dating for the foreseeable future and two, never get involved with another musician for as long as I live." Because obviously, she couldn't trust herself. And dating musicians only muddied her professional life.

Haley stopped in front of the sofa and tipped back her head, setting her gaze toward the balcony. "Gorgeous. I bet it'll look even better at night."

"I'm sure it will." They'd wrapped the windows in fairy lights as well. "We won't need the lamps once we have trees in here."

"That's the goal." Haley winked. "You know, if you rule out musicians you are limiting yourself to an accountant or pharmacist or rocket scientist."

"Bring it. I want someone with a nine-to-five."

"Not someone who can travel with you?"

"Nope." She pointed at her mouth. "Never. Again."

Haley laughed, clearly unoffended. "I hear you."

The insurance adjuster arrived, and Kate showed him her car in the garage. He took photos from all angles and entered notes on his tablet. "I'll get back to you soon."

"Sounds good. Thanks for coming out. Any news on the truck that hit me?" She could ask Zach herself, but they'd agreed to keep this accident stuff out of their conversations.

"We're working with him. But don't worry, you'll only have to pay your deductible. The rest is covered, even if your station wagon is totaled."

The bright side of that? A newer vehicle. That wouldn't be all bad.

She watched him walk to his SUV and then back out of the driveway. Soon, this whole accident mess would be behind her.

Later that evening, Kate craved peace and comfort. So many changes lately were taking a toll. "I'm up for another movie tonight. You?"

"Let's cook dinner and then watch a Christmas special. I'm done in."

"Me too."

Over a light meal of broiled chicken breasts, brown rice, and steamed carrots, Kate knew she needed to admit one more thing. "I didn't tell Heath this, but I haven't written anything for the new album yet."

"You haven't? You're always composing. When did you stop?" Haley's unnerved expression inflated Kate's insecurities.

"The last piece was . . . hmm. Back in April?" Normally, she didn't let herself get alarmed, but admitting that aloud unsettled her.

"That's a long time. Are you concerned? I mean, your well of inspiration doesn't usually run dry." Where was the encouraging Haley?

Kate's palms sweated. She reached for her ice water, gripped the glass tightly, and took a sip. What if she couldn't produce like she used to? "Your questions are freaking me out. Got any solutions?"

Haley grinned, clearly not letting anxiety eat at her. Good. Maybe that monster shouldn't gnaw on Kate either. "Sorry about that. I'm thinking."

"To answer your question, I haven't been too stressed out. I've had dry spells before."

Another topic Kate didn't want to discuss popped into her mind, along with clarity. "I think it was the accident last spring."

Haley set down her fork. "We haven't talked about that much lately."

"I know." Her mind tracked back to tailgating Zach. "This 'not trusting my own judgment' runs deep. I'm uninspired and wondering if that's my fate. If I can't compose a slew of unique pieces by mid- to late December, I'll need to tell Beth at least. Maybe she should give it a try. Or maybe Nelson, but he's already told us he doesn't read music beyond chord charts. He's not adept at making use of staff paper, not to mention writing for bass, tenor, and treble clefs."

"Here's a crazy idea. I say you invite Zach to join in cowriting. You sure made magic the other night. I mean, it was otherworldly, girl."

Kate bit her lip. She couldn't argue with that. Still, hers was a solo process. "Nah, you know I always write alone, at least at first. It's too vulnerable to invite someone else into that place."

"It's not like you add lyrics and pen love songs. Just think about it, okay? You often rule things out too fast, shutting down ideas. Allow this to be a season when you expand a bit. Try something new." Haley let that comment resonate in the quiet room.

Could she permit someone else access to her songwriting process? Just because she'd always done something one way didn't mean she had to continue to do so.

Haley gathered some dishes to tote to the dishwasher. "It'll be fun to have Zach and Topher over here tomorrow night."

Kate picked up her plate and silverware and moved to the sink. "I've been thinking about them. You know, I could stay all stuck in my troubles, but what good is that? I'd rather help someone else this season. So, while I'm in town, I'm going to see if I can help Topher."

"Except, you'll be busy at the piano and Topher doesn't know you. *I'll* get through to Topher. You focus on music. Let's see what happens with that."

"Zach hasn't asked for help at church."

"Well, I think he will. And when he does, remember, you're trying new things, looking for ways to bless others. Not shutting down people and their suggestions."

"I'll try." The more her life felt out of control, the more she longed to pin something—

anything–down.

"Hon, we all have seasons where we're between sure things and need a little push in this direction or that one. This is one of those seasons for you." Haley reached for Kate's arm. "You launched a musical group. You've made tons of correct decisions. Don't let Heath's hang-ups rob you of your confidence. Now, I'll make the popcorn, you load the dishwasher. Let's get to relaxing."

Kate rinsed the first plate. "Sounds good."

She could use the distraction and the friend time, because right now, her mind spun with thoughts of Zach coming back over and her need to work this season. Was it crazy to consider writing together?

Eight

Cello and piano music rode along with Zach and his son Saturday night. Again, Topher wasn't talking. Zach debated calling off their evening plans, but that might break Topher's heart. No, he'd keep his word. But he sincerely hoped, for the sake of their hostesses, that Toph wouldn't be sullen once they arrived.

Zach had decided to contribute cinnamon rolls. Store bought. Picked up on the way home from work. They'd probably understand.

"Best behavior, bud, okay? The house is nice, and we don't want to wreck anything."

No response. Zach ran through the list of possible things bothering his son. They talked about his mother. Zach thought Topher had found peace around that. He seemed fine with school, but Zach would learn more next week when he met with the counselor. And Topher still wouldn't answer questions related to his moodiness.

"Okay?" he repeated. Though frustration rose, Zach tried to keep his tone light. He didn't want to bully his kid into responding. He'd try a different approach. "What are you most looking forward to?"

"Will Miss Kate play the cello again?"

Ah, he speaks. "Yes. I mean, that's the plan. And I'll play piano." Something *Zach* anticipated. Plus, he had a request to make.

"I like listening to her music. It reminds me of this." Toph pointed at the old truck's radio/CD player.

"Just because Miss Kate plays a cello doesn't mean she's the same cellist. Lots of people play that instrument. But you're right, Toph. A cello, guitar, voice, and piano make up this group." Zach could check out the group's website, but he hadn't had time lately. What were the odds they were the same person? Nearly impossible, so why bother? And he didn't watch the group's videos. He preferred to listen to, not watch, his music.

"I don't hear any words."

"True. A singer uses her voice as her instrument. I like how musical you are, Son."

They pulled into the driveway, and Zach parked next to the garage so he wouldn't block the door. He climbed out, grabbing the store-bought pan of rolls. Topher joined him with a bit of enthusiasm in his posture. Maybe there was hope.

At the entrance, Zach knocked.

"I like how musical Miss Kate is," Topher echoed Zach's words, peering up at him. "She'd make a great momma."

Zach gave his son a double take. "Wha—?"

"Welcome!" Haley swung open the door, and Zach cleared his expression. A wash of warm air smelling of pizza dough and tomato sauce engulfed him. That frozen burrito he'd eaten hours ago couldn't compete. His stomach rumbled loudly, which he covered by directing Toph to step inside and remove his shoes. The kiddo's socks didn't match, and Zach sighed. His son needed a mother who could look out for things like that. Zach had enough trouble focusing on their survival and maybe doing laundry once every two weeks. It wasn't that he couldn't do it, or even that he thought it was beneath him. He just didn't take the time for it, and it didn't occur to him to plan ahead, until moments like this when embarrassment harassed him. Hannah had always looked after Topher's clothes.

Had his son really implied he'd like Kate as a new mother? Was that what ate at him? He'd never said anything like that until today.

"We're glad you guys came." Haley reached for Topher's hand, letting him make the decision whether to go with her or not. He cooperated. "I want to show you what we did to the living room since you were here last." She glanced over her shoulder at Zach as she led Topher away. "Join Kate in the kitchen? She's elbow-deep in dinner prep."

Zach made his way toward delicious aromas, aluminum tray of rolls in hand.

"Hi Miss Kate!" Topher called as Haley brought him into the great room.

"Hey, Topher. I'm glad you're here."

"Me too." His face glowed as he interacted with Kate, and Zach marveled. "Wow. The mansion is a Christmas wonderland." Topher spun, head tipped back and eyes wide.

"You've been busy." Zach gestured toward the Christmassy décor, but his attention swung to Kate who stood at the closest island wearing an apron over a long maroon sweater and dark blue skinny jeans. Her light brown hair was up in a messy bun and she had a smudge of flour on her forehead, which didn't surprise him, given the state of her hands. The whole effect? Cute.

He'd made a promise to himself though—to keep his distance. This visit was about feeding his son, both physically and emotionally. For some reason, the cello spoke to him. Did he remember his grandmother playing it? She'd done so less often as she'd grown older. Topher's mom, Zach's late wife had played too. Did Topher remember that? Was that part of the connection Topher made with Kate?

Of course Topher's request, if he'd meant it as Zach assumed, was absurd. As lonely as the two of them may be, Zach couldn't promise any new mommies in Topher's immediate future.

The second reason for visiting was to make his request about Christmas music for church. That was it. Nothing personal or involved. Tell that to the part of him watching Kate smile directly at him while brushing a lock of hair from her forehead with a flour-dusted knuckle. That part went speechless. He shifted his attention to his son and Haley.

The great room's clear Christmas lights reflected off the piano, and Topher was right. It was magical—not that Zach believed in magic anymore. His wife had *made* Christmas with all the decorations and baking, including a cake for Jesus's birthday. She'd finish a day of teaching at the elementary school and spend an hour or two creating treats. Her students enjoyed them. Zach loved how she thought of comforts and celebrating each season. Of course Topher would miss that, would miss her. But why the suggestion about Kate if he missed Hannah?

That feeling of magical Christmases, those days, were well behind them. Theirs was still survival mode. *Do well at my job. Please the senior pastor and the congregation. Feed and clothe my son—preferably with clean clothes and matching socks. Try to reach him. Sell a slew of Christmas trees. Stay healthy, for my son. Pay my medical bills and insurance deductible.* He'd stay focused on those goals and ignore his attraction to the woman standing a few feet away.

Peaceful musical strains filled the great

room from hidden speakers. Was that . . . ? "Which group is this?" He faced Kate, who focused toward the counter covered in pizza makings but didn't answer.

"That's Prism Effect," Haley called from the living area. She led Toph around and let him explore the decorations. Zach liked seeing the joy on his son's face.

"We love that band, huh, Dad?" Topher said, peering up at Haley and then over at Zach. "We play them in the car. Dad has them on his phone too."

Kate gave Zach a glimpse of her face as if she knew something he didn't. He shrugged. "I know good music when I hear it, what can I say?" He pointed at himself. "Music director."

"Um, Kate, what do you think of this ensemble?" Haley's words seemed like a nudge, even from twenty feet away. But Zach couldn't see why.

Kate busied herself rearranging the bowls of toppings on the granite-covered bar. Huh. What made her uncomfortable? "I've spent hours listening to these songs myself," she finally said.

"Good taste." Zach washed his hands at the prep sink, drying them on a paper towel. Then, he faced Kate again. She spread sauce over the second of two large partially baked pizza crusts. The first pie contained pineapple and ham, from what he could tell. He found browned ground beef, green peppers, mushrooms, onions, and black olives in small dishes around the island. Shredded mozzarella lay mounded on a plate.

"I like how original the compositions are," Zach said, loudly enough to be heard in the living area. "And that the cello leads out." Kate met his eyes so he admitted, "Favorite instrument. I wonder if they only do originals and if so, which members write the music." The melodies genuinely spoke to him as if Prism Effect *did* include lyrics. How the composers did that, he didn't know. He was better at choir directing and lining up pieces for a church concert than the mechanics of composing.

"I like that the singer doesn't use words," Topher said, and Zach grinned with pride. Smart kid liked to show off what his dad had just taught him. "Her voice is her instrument."

Haley exchanged a glance with Kate who finished with the sauce. "That's right, Toph. The whole group is full of talented people," Haley said. "I've heard that the main composer is the cello player, to answer your question, Zach."

Kate wiped her smeared hands on a paper towel. "So, Zach, Topher, what are your favorite pizza toppings? The only thing I didn't get out was the pepperoni, but we do have some."

Haley released Topher's hand, and he darted over to the island where he checked the array of options with oohs and aahs and a couple of jumps. Soon, he'd selected nearly everything. He never had liked mushrooms.

"How about half and half?" Zach's side would include what Hannah had always called "sliced fungus." He finished spreading the sauce on their crust and picked up the small bowl of ground beef and a teaspoon.

"Go for it." Kate pointed at her pizza. "I'll get ours into the top oven, and you guys can bake yours in the second one."

Zach divided the pie into two, visually, and spread the ingredients over it. He used a line of sliced black olives down the middle to keep it obvious.

Haley showed Topher the gingerbread house kit in the corner of the kitchen. "What do you think?"

His face lit up again. Something about

being here, with these women, especially with Haley taking a special interest in him, and the kid opened up. "But I also want to hear the music when they start playing." Topher hooked a thumb behind him, toward where Zach and Kate worked. Kate wiped down the granite as Zach reached for the cheese.

"Don't worry," Haley reassured him. "Their music will fill this whole house."

Kate peered through the glass into the oven. They'd left the conversation of Prism Effect, and she could relax again. She'd never liked when people made a fuss over her or her ac-complishments. Haley said that was silly—she should "bask." She grinned, remembering how her BFF sang the word. Kate just wanted to hang out with these new friends. Still, that look of appreciation in Zach's eyes now and then did touch her.

It was probably best he hear it from Kate, because knowing Haley, she wasn't going to let it drop.

The cheese had almost browned enough on the pizza the women would share. Zach and

Topher's would need a few more minutes. "Hey, when do you guys plan to leave tonight?" She kept her voice low so as not to disturb Haley and Topher who told stories on the white sofa. "I want to make sure we have enough time for everything."

"Probably eight or eight-thirty. Sunday mornings start early for us."

"Gotcha." She pulled her pizza from the top oven and set it on the back counter's wooden cutting board. "Couple more minutes. Do you want to pour drinks?"

"Sure. Soda? Water?"

"Water all around is fine with us. But we do have soda, if you prefer." She pointed toward the fridge while she stood guard at the oven, mitts covering each hand.

He pulled out a can of Coke and filled water glasses from the fridge door. He set the cups around the table. "Thanks again for having us over this week—twice."

"Our pleasure." Somehow their girls' weekend had morphed a bit, but right now, with his pine scent wafting toward her, she didn't mind. "I'm looking forward to playing tonight."

"Me too." Something about that handsome

face turned her way. Sincerity. Perhaps a hint of timidity.

She pulled out the second pie. "Okay with this cheese color?"

"As long as it's melted, it's perfect."

"Finished." She gave a decisive nod and set the baking sheet down next to a slicer. "Let's cool these for a minute."

"Good plan. I'll get Topher's on a plate, so it has an advantage." He grabbed the tool and divided up the disk. "You know, I would have guessed Prism Effect would be one of your favorite groups, since you play the cello. I mean, between them and the Piano Guys, with their amazing cellist, they are rock stars."

She nodded.

"What is it you do for a day job?" He raised his brows in her direction. "I can't believe I never asked you that."

"I'm a professional musician. Like you."

"At a church, or . . . ?"

"Traveling." Still she hesitated to divulge the truth. Her news would change their dynamic, and she liked things as they were. "Hey guys, it's about time to eat. Want to wash up?" she called to Haley and Topher. After they'd meandered to the hall bathroom sink, she said, "Confession? Before those two join us?"

Zach gave her his attention, standing nearby with Topher's plate in his hands. He set it down on the granite. "Go for it."

"I saw you on the ferry, listening to Prism Effect, humming along while you waited to pay for your drink."

"You did? I didn't see you."

"Yeah, you were wrapped up in it. And... it meant something to me."

He cocked a hip against the counter. "Why?"

Deep breath. "I'm the cellist in the group."

He swallowed. "You are? That's you?" Admiration filled his features, and she drank it in, her face going hot. "I should have known. But, why not tell us?"

"I didn't want to make a big deal." She waved at nothing. "All that attention."

"Topher's gonna freak," Zach whispered as the noises grew louder from the hall. "If you're okay with telling him."

She fiddled with the server and spoon rest on the counter. "I don't want things to change. I'm just me."

He studied her, a new *something* in his expression.

"That look." She pointed at his face. "That's the one I'm talking about." Although, it wasn't all bad.

"What if I promise not to treat you any differently than I have been?"

"Well, let's see." She tipped her head. "You've been respectful, kind, polite, and…" And a bit protective, but she didn't add that, though she'd noticed at the accident and afterward. Even now, he seemed interested in her comfort. Huh. So unlike Heath. "And professional. I could live with more of that."

"Good." That admiration nudged up a notch.

And, despite herself, she liked it.

Nine

Topher flipped with the news, just as Zach knew he would. "You're the cellist we keep listening to? Dad! Did you know that?"

Zach loved seeing his enthusiasm, but he didn't want Kate to feel uncomfortable or to regret letting them in on her secret. "I just found out, buddy. But she's still Miss Kate to us, and we're still friends. It doesn't change anything." He glanced at Kate for confirmation. *Back me up here?*

She nodded, catching on. "Yes, we're still friends, okay, kiddo?"

Topher went quiet, chewing on another bite of his loaded pizza. "But I thought famous people were . . . different."

Kate licked her lips, napkin rising to her face as if she was trying to cover a smile. Zach waited her out because his mouth was full of food. And he was curious what she'd say.

"Like, because they're famous they don't talk to just anybody?" Kate asked Topher, meeting his eyes.

"Yeah, or they're never where normal people are."

"Well, Topher, here's a secret for you. Ready?"

Zach grinned. His son set his pizza down, eyes wide, nodding. It seemed Kate and her ensemble were just the distraction Topher needed, and Zach could kiss her for her kindness to his son. His mind tripped off into a fantasy of kissing her hand like some knight, but he quickly brought himself back.

"Famous people are just regular people, like you and your dad." She gave Zach a smile and he relished the moment of her personal focus, feeling perhaps like his son in that moment. A bit starstruck. He might have a sprinkle of that stardust in his own eyes.

Though he'd tried not to flip out, it had shifted his world to know he was baking up pizzas with the cellist from Prism Effect. That he'd played carols with her on Wednesday and would again tonight. Crazy! He'd never fanboyed, in person, for any musician. Sure, he'd looked up to people for their talent, maybe had a crush or two on female artists in his youth. But sitting down to dinner with someone he admired this much? Not until this week.

Given her fame, asking her to put on a free concert at their church seemed silly now. Famous cellists didn't make local churches their holiday hangouts. They did professional gigs, for which they were paid. Well. But his church didn't pay their participants. The goal was for musicians to voluntarily offer a Christmas Eve concert for the community. So, he'd leave off mentioning it to her.

"I like that you're regular, Miss Kate. And I want to hear you play something."

"Soon, buddy," Zach said, putting a hand on his son's shoulder. Anticipation tingled through him. "I mean, if Miss Kate still wants to."

She gave Zach a mock scolding face, well it was subtle, but he still read it. "I absolutely still do."

"Great," Zach and Topher said in unison.

"Now, who's ready for some of those cinnamon rolls you two brought?"

"I'll warm them up," Haley said, gathering plates and hustling across the room toward the far sink.

Minutes later, they sat pulling apart the gooey rolls, the fragrance of cinnamon replacing the aroma of tomatoes and cheese in the house.

"So, is your church putting on a Christmas program?" Kate asked.

Well, he hadn't meant to go here. "Yes, we are. One part of the performance will be with the kids' choir. But I'd like to put on a little concert, including a bell choir, if I can find enough volunteers. Still trying to find performers." He pinched off another bite of roll. "And no, I am not fishing for you to volunteer. Not at all."

"Oh, I didn't think so." Without adding anything else, Kate sipped her cocoa. Good. Haley leaned toward Kate and nudged her with her elbow, but Kate didn't seem to take the bait.

"Are you two going to play together now?" Topher piped up.

"Yes." Zach exhaled, glad for a chance to

end this awkward moment. "I think it's time."

"Let's wash our hands, buddy." Haley took Topher to the prep sink in the island.

"Good idea." Kate nodded toward the other sink, and Zach met her there.

Moments later, Haley and Toph had taken up seats on the white sofa, an attentive audience.

Kate disappeared into the den and returned with her cello. She seemed to have no problem toting that monster. Another reason he admired her. Her strength. She'd mastered her instrument. And she didn't look for kudos from anybody in order to feel validated or worthwhile. She carried an air of humility in the way she seemed oblivious to how beautiful she was, with her silken brown hair and blue-gray eyes. He never saw her messing with her locks or posing. She simply went about the kitchen or the living area as if she truly wasn't trying to attract attention. But awareness kept drawing his focus back to her.

"You okay, Dad?" Topher sounded impatient to get to the music.

From her perch, where she'd settled the cello's endpin between her feet, Kate leaned toward Toph, as well as she could. "Any requests?"

"Play a Christmas song!" Topher directed from the front row.

"Yes, play a carol," Haley echoed, wearing a big grin.

"'O, Holy Night'?" Kate suggested. "Key of D?"

"Sounds good." Zach rarely needed to check his fingerings. As a kid he'd watched blind professional pianists perform expertly and he'd determined that he'd be able to play by feel, as well as by ear. Tonight, he took the melody and Kate embellished. Zach leaned in to the music. Eyes closed. Relishing the harmonies like a favorite dessert. Like when he'd put Topher to bed, grab his earbuds, and indulge in Prism Effect's music after a long day.

He opened his eyes and studied Kate's effortless expertise.

Yeah, there might be stardust.

Ten

Maybe it was the reflection of the twinkle lights off the glistening white piano. Maybe it was the music they made together. Or maybe it was the way Zach lost himself in the experience. He seemed to let the music carry him wherever it wanted, as if abandoned to it. He'd tip his head back, and an expression of sheer pleasure came over him. Swept away. And the longer she watched him the more caught up she became. Christmas magic or something else?

Noticing his strong jaw and that five o'clock shadow wasn't helping, or the way his sweater hugged his arms and shoulders. His movements as he played... Heath could never compare. Zach drew her.

They finished the carol to applause from their audience.

"Do another one!" Topher called from the white sofa.

Zach offered a backdrop for Kate's melody work on "Joy to the World."

Cheering ensued when they wrapped up that song, and Kate set her cello on its stand. "Need. Water," she joked, before marching to the kitchen. "You want some?" she asked Zach.

"Yes, thanks."

Haley and Topher scrambled up onto bar stools and opened the gingerbread house kit. Topher squeezed the sealed bags of frosting, one in each hand.

Zach joined them in the kitchen. He wore an expression of enjoyment as he glanced around the room, toward her and the others. Contentment, maybe? She handed him his glass.

"So, how long are you in town?" he asked after taking the water with a thanks. "Through Christmas, you think?"

"Yes, thankfully." Her savings would keep her for a while. But she needed to make some serious decisions about what was next, and her aversion to Heath clouded that. To keep her commitment to her band, she must find inspiration and get some notes down on staff paper. And she needed to line up housing post-holiday season.

"Moving in with Haley here?" He gestured toward the mansion.

"I'm renting here, and Haley is headed back to her apartment." Part of Kate felt guilty. This house was a luxury for one person. But what if God wanted her here? Who was she to say no to His generosity? Plus, Haley's parents were glad to have someone they trusted rent long term. Zach seemed to be fishing around the topic of his Christmas program, and she was at peace with leaving it up to him to ask her, if he still wanted.

Zach glanced upward and about the great room. "The acoustics in this space are perfect. Haley said you do most of the composing for your ensemble."

"True." She'd tried co-writing with Heath a few times, but he criticized often. Admittedly, he didn't do well with anything cooperative, unless it garnered him a heap of accolades. It was as if he had no room for her in the process. They worked better apart.

Fitting.

Following a few swigs, Zach set his glass on the counter. "Have you ever found a writing partner who complements your work?"

"Um, compliments or complements?" She emphasized the subtle vowel sounds.

His eyes twinkled as if he'd be happy to offer compliments if she asked. "Both."

"Not yet."

"Well, having played several songs with you this week, and having enjoyed Prism Effect for years, I admit your work inspires me and . . . I don't know. Ministers to me?" He closed his eyes. "That sounds corny. But it's probably the best way to say it." He shrugged. "Church guy."

Her heart melted a little at his vulnerability and deep honesty. "No, I get it, being a church person myself. And wow, no one's ever said that to me before. Thank you."

"As for complement," he began, emphasizing the short *e* sound, "I thought we were rather complementary of each other, supporting without overshadowing. Leaving room for artistry."

"I agree." *Have you found someone to write with?* Maybe.

For her, the creative part of her brain

connected with her heart. Love inspired her. Relationship. Life. Beauty in creation. Heath's rejection made a desert of her creative inner place. The last two music sessions with Zach? Inspiring.

She took in his dark hair, the shimmer in his soft, hazel eyes from these reflective Christmas lights. They weren't alone, but it almost seemed like they were. "Do you write music, Zach? Obviously you're talented and musically minded, like your son, I noticed."

Zach beamed. "He is, isn't he?"

She wanted to ask about Topher's mother, but wouldn't risk chasing Zach's smile away. Neither one of them ever mentioned her, so was she living elsewhere? Zach didn't wear a ring, but Kate had known plenty of married men who didn't, especially musicians. Maybe they were divorced, which wasn't unheard of in her church circles. She'd liked his reference to music ministering to someone. His involvement there wasn't just a job to him.

"Yes, I write. Nothing like your pieces, of course. Nothing four-part. Just worship choruses, anthemic so people can experience Him. A few love songs, years ago."

Ah, he was a romantic. Shoot. Learning new

things about him only drew her more. She was beginning to see the inner workings of that guy on the ferry who lost himself to her compositions. Hard to believe he was the same guy from the accident. But everyone made mistakes.

"Why did the music stop?" Topher climbed down, project half-finished on the counter. "Can you play again? Maybe do one of the songs we listen to in Dad's truck, Miss Kate?"

"Sure. Which one?"

Topher hummed a couple of measures of one of Kate's favorite tracks. "I know that one." She glanced at Zach. "Join me?" He played by feel. Did he play by ear too?

Sure enough, he did. He'd memorized the piano part, but he embellished. The atmosphere changed again. Electricity crackled in the air. Zach met her eyes this time, not closing his, meeting her in the music. Intoxicating.

Caught up, halfway through the second chorus, she glanced at Topher to see his joy but found him standing there, tears silently streaming down his face, shoulders shaking. She froze, cello music stalled, and gave Zach a look, dipping her head toward his son, who stood behind him.

He spun, the piano notes stopping abruptly. "Toph." He was at his son's side in a blur.

Kate rushed to prop her instrument on its stand out of the way and get closer. "What happened?"

The poor, clearly heartbroken kid didn't answer. He just stood there, with Zach's hands on his shoulders, while his dad checked him over. Had Topher eaten too much? Did his stomach ache?

Haley rushed from the kitchen side of the great room. "Oh, no." She took a position beside Kate, no doubt feeling just as helpless.

"Did he fall?" Zach asked Haley.

"No, he was fine. I thought he was enjoying the music and just wanted to be closer."

"Me too," Kate put in. "He seemed okay for a while."

Topher didn't answer his dad's repeated questions.

Kate knelt in front of him. "Hey kiddo, could you tell us what happened? Why are you crying?" Was it okay to ask a little boy that question, or would he stay silent out of embarrassment? What did she know of raising a child? Maybe he hadn't gotten the message that boys didn't cry just yet. Zach seemed level-headed, not over-the-top "men don't cry." And, seriously, to play that passionately, the man had to be at least a little in touch with his feelings. She glanced at him. He was all care for his son, brows furrowed, kneeling, eyes full of concern.

Her heart tugged. *What a picture.*

She refocused on Topher. "Please tell me? Was it the music?"

Topher looked between his father and Kate and then Haley and back to Kate. Instead of speaking, he grunted and bolted toward the front door, pushing against the hallway Christmas tree on his way by. A glass ornament fell off and crashed to the hardwoods, shattering. Glass shards scattered. Topher froze. Haley darted for the broom closet. None of them wore shoes. Kate reached into the closet and threw on the first pair of boots she could find over her fluffy socks. Of course, none of the women's footwear in there would fit Zach or Topher.

"Be careful everyone," Haley called.

Kate put the broom Haley handed her to work.

Still sock-footed, Zach scooped up his son and carried him, stepping gingerly around the remnants.

"Now that Topher is safe, maybe you should stand still until I get this swept up, Zach. Please," Kate suggested.

He stopped halfway down the hall, holding Topher tighter as if he could shield him from further danger. She ran the broom over the floor, hearing some of Zach's parental lecture to his son. "I'm sorry you're in pain, but you need to apologize to Miss Haley and Miss Kate. Shoving the tree was dangerous."

Kate wanted to say that it was okay, but one, this wasn't her house. And two, was it acceptable to interrupt a father to let his son off the hook? Probably not. She swept together the glass, all that she could see, and even reached the broom's brush into far spots to ensure she got what might be hiding behind the ficus and in doorways off the hall.

"Okay, it's probably safe now." She stood guard over the pile she'd collected and planned to get the dustpan as soon as they left, followed by a vacuum cleaner for running over this entire floor. Her heart broke for Topher. What must be eating him that he'd burst into tears while they played?

If only he'd tell someone . . . they could do

something.

How often did she keep her fears and worries bottled up, without talking to the Lord about them, without "casting her cares" as her favorite verse said?

Please, Lord, help Topher unburden himself soon.

Eleven

I need your help. He won't talk to me." In late November, Zach launched into his spiel almost before the school counselor, Cathy McMurray, had a chance to take her seat behind the desk. She was probably twenty years Zach's senior and had a counselor's persona—kind, compassionate, competent. He got a warm maternal vibe from her, and for some reason that comforted him. Crazy. He was a grown man, but Topher's pain made Zach vulnerable. He hoped she could help them.

No matter how gently Zach tried to coax him, Topher wouldn't talk about his outburst, wouldn't explain himself. Even when Zach mentioned Topher's suggestion that Kate would make a great mother, a topic Zach would rather not bring up, Toph remained silent. But if Kate playing the cello like his late mother hadn't been the connection, what could it have been? On a calm day, when Zach asked him whether he remembered his mom playing an instrument, Topher couldn't recall it.

"I understand, Mr. Tillmon. His teacher has also expressed some concern. Has anything happened since the school year began that may be the cause? A move? A loss? A big change in his life—diagnosis, new baby, foster child in the family, death of a beloved pet, adoption?"

"Nothing like that." He'd already run through a similar list in his head, always scrambling for answers. And he hadn't said a thing about his doctor's visits, so Topher couldn't know about the possibility of Zach having skin cancer.

Cathy leaned forward, hands folded on her desk. She wore a simple gold wedding ring, and her graying hair was styled professionally. The two of them had met before, but Topher had been fine then. Of course, that was in August when the kiddo had been cheerful and adventurous. "It's possible he's missing his mother and doesn't know how to express it. You mentioned she died three years ago?"

"Yes, but when I ask him about her I don't see any light bulbs."

"Since it's been that long, he has probably processed some of his pain, which means we may be looking for something else, especially if he talks openly about her."

"He does." Should Zach mention Topher's comment about a new mother? "We just met a family friend, who plays cello like my late wife. Is it possible Topher is unconsciously connecting the two of them? He says he doesn't remember his mom playing an instrument, but maybe part of him does."

"That's interesting." Cathy made a note on a legal pad in front of her. "Let's not rule that out. Has he ever acted like this before?"

Another good question. "Always around the holidays and only for the past few years. But it's much worse this time. He tends to snap out of it in January or February."

"If I may, and I'm sorry if this brings up painful memories, but is there any chance his mother died during the fall, three years ago?"

"She did, but I didn't think, given how young Topher was at the time, that he'd make that connection." His cell buzzed with a text alert. He tugged out his phone. "One second."

"Of course." Cathy went back to jotting notes.

PLEASE CALL OUR MEDICAL OFFICES AT YOUR EARLIEST CONVENIENCE.

He'd been dreading word of his test results. Right now, he needed to focus on his son. He pocketed his phone.

"Everything all right?" Compassion shone in the counselor's gaze.

"It will be. So, what's next? How do I help him?"

"We will come up with a plan. If you're interested, I'll put you in touch with a children's therapist who can work with him."

"If he won't talk to me, why would he talk to a stranger?"

Cathy faced him and adjusted her glasses. "I say it's worth trying. One of us will get through to him."

"Okay, let's give it a shot." Zach headed out into the hallway a few minutes later, unsure if this appointment had helped or not. But it was clear that professionals were needed if they were going to solve the mystery of his son's despondency.

Kate ran her bow over the strings, filling the great room with music. Birch Harbor's sparkling blue water inspired her this morning. Maybe she'd write a playful staccato piece to mimic the sounds of water dripping or cascading.

She'd settled into a routine living alone here the past couple of weeks. Haley popped in now and then, but she'd returned to her apartment. They'd shared a peaceful Thanksgiving in the mansion last Thursday.

Despite all her attempts to reach out to Zach about pitching Haley's idea that they write together, he didn't respond. Of course, he must be busy with Topher. Strange how the kiddo could seem sullen and then excited to explore the Christmas decorations or make gingerbread houses. He loved the music, but in some way it seemed to torment him. Did he not understand his emotions himself? It would be frustrating if even he couldn't put it into words. No one could blame him.

Maybe she should mention that revelation

to Zach. Would it help? A couple weeks had passed since they'd visited and Topher had his breakdown. Could be Zach already knew what she was only now figuring out. Kate wasn't a mom. She'd had younger siblings but had never been a teacher or nanny. Haley was great with kids. She might have some input. They were sharing a late lunch before Haley's work shift.

An hour later, when Haley arrived, the only thing Kate had penciled in on her staff paper was a possible title.

Haley plopped a couple of cloth, reusable shopping bags onto the counter. "When do you get your car back from the shop?"

Kate set her cello in its stand and joined Haley in the kitchen. "Another few days. Glad for the rental, though there's no way my cello would fit in the back of that teensy, tiny car."

"Good thing you're not touring now." Haley set her keys and purse aside. "How goes the writing?"

"Terribly. I'm uninspired. Blocked." A wave of anxiety stole over her. What if she never wrote again? "I'll help. One sec." She washed her hands.

"I picked up a chicken for us to roast."

They unpacked broccoli and baby red potatoes. Haley rarely did things the usual way. Why not have a big meal in the middle of the day? "I'm sure it'll turn around soon." She scrubbed the potatoes under water at the prep sink.

Kate found a roasting pan and turned the top oven on to preheat to 375 degrees. They'd roast this for two hours, filling the house with the aroma. Haley could take a container of leftovers to work for her break tonight. And Kate would eat a few scraps with carrot sticks for dinner. "I hope so."

"I've given you my suggestion, and I'll leave it at that." Haley switched to cleaning the broccoli, spritzing it with a vegetable wash spray and rinsing it under the faucet.

Kate placed the whole chicken, white meat side down, in the roasting pan and liberally sprinkled seasoning salt all over it. "I'd appreciate it." Especially since she meant for Kate to inconvenience Zach.

Over the meal, Kate shared her ideas about Topher, and Haley seemed to agree. Now, Kate wanted to tell Zach. "Does he answer your texts?"

"Nope. And I haven't had a chance to talk

with him at church the last couple of weeks. I'm surprised you haven't cornered him."

Kate shrugged. "It's awkward. I don't want to make him uncomfortable. I mean, he's on the job."

Haley swallowed her latest bite, watching Kate closely. "You like him."

"I'm drawn to him, but, Hales, I just broke up with Heath. I'd rather keep my distance from guys right now."

"Can't blame you, I guess." Haley pointed her empty fork across the table. "But you two sound amazing together."

No arguing with that.

The aroma of savory roasted chicken still filled the house, and the meat was so tender, it fell off the bone. As the room darkened, Haley left her plate and meandered around clicking on all the Christmas lights. She'd leave for work soon.

Back in the kitchen, she toted her dishes to the sink. "How will you work with Heath again?"

"No idea. You don't suppose we could fire him, do you?" Kate could hope for an easy solution, not that they'd find one. She helped clear the table.

"Maybe he'll volunteer to leave." Haley rinsed plates and set them in the dishwasher.

"That would be a dream, except, then, we'd have to find a new pianist we all get along with." She really should talk with her fellow group mates about this problem, but she wouldn't want Heath to find out and then feel they'd ganged up on him.

"Any chance that Heath will try to turn the others against you, that *they'd* fire *you*?"

"I started Prism Effect. Where it goes, I go. Plus, Beth and Nelson have been more in my corner than his. But if we can't figure this out, and if I never write again, we're doomed." Kate didn't want to think about starting over. Those worries kept her up some nights. The public shame of losing her position, the insecurity of whether or not she could launch a new ensemble with a new name. She didn't want to give up all she'd worked hard for. "Ugh, it's scary."

"For sure. You'll need to be certain before you make any changes. It's nice you have this holiday season to rethink your life." Haley wiped her hands and then peeked at her phone, which had been lying upside down on the island. "Oops, I need to run and change for work. Do you mind finishing cleanup?"

"Not at all. Thanks for listening, Hales."

"You got it." They hugged and Haley scooted off to the bathroom with her backpack.

Kate didn't look forward to another lonely evening in this big house, as beautiful as it was. Sometimes she could be so discontent. *I'm sorry, Lord. Thank You for letting me spend the holiday season here. Please fill up my empty spaces with Your love.* Reaching out to Zach would at least give her a sense of helping someone else, not getting too bogged down in her own problems.

The house was silent after her friend left. Kate queued up her last album on her MP3 player. But she wanted something Christmassy, so she switched to the Piano Guys. Their skills impressed her. Yeah, she had a ways to go to measure up to her ideal.

She'd also always dreamed of doing a Christmas album, but would there be a market for it? They'd have to set themselves apart. And of course, it was too late to do a whole album for *this* Christmas.

Thirty minutes later, another glance around the opulent kitchen proved she'd made every surface gleam. She settled in the living room on the white sofa and pulled out her phone. How to bring up her epiphany with Zach? No guarantee he'd answer his cell, but would he answer the church's phone?

The clock read 3:30, which meant Topher was likely out of school. Zach had mentioned working morning to midday office hours, and then switching to his second job at a local Christmas tree farm to help pay the bills. Poor guy. And his son was suffering, which must only be adding to his stress.

No one answered the church's main number, so she'd go to plan B. But rather than call him and risk his son overhearing, she'd send a text that Topher probably wouldn't see. HEY, ZACH, IT'S KATE. I WONDERED IF I COULD SHARE AN IDEA I HAD WITH YOU. IT'S NOT URGENT, BUT MAYBE I CAN HELP. WOULD YOU BE OPEN TO THAT? IF NOT, I'LL MIND MY OWN BUSINESS. OH, THIS IS ABOUT OUR LAST GET-TOGETHER.

She wouldn't type in Topher's name, and she'd leave it vague in case the seven-year-old saw it.

Her phone rang almost immediately. "Hey, Kate."

She liked that tone in his voice. Gentle. Warm. Low. Whew. She'd forgotten what he sounded like after the last couple of weeks. "Hi. That was quick. You must have read my text."

"Confession?" he asked like she'd done with him. "I'm sitting here in my truck playing Prism Effect while I worry about my son."

That admission sent a zing through her. "My revelation is about him. Want to hear it?"

"Better idea—if you're free."

"I'm free. What's up?"

"Could I drop by for a visit? I need to chat with you about something too."

"Sure. Where's Topher?"

"At my sister's."

"C'mon over."

Twelve

The sky had grown dark by the time Zach pulled into Kate's driveway. He'd seen her at church, but he'd kept his distance. He hadn't wanted anyone to get too close, ask too many questions, not with the way his life unraveled. Medical news. Bills. Topher's instability. And Zach's sister prying. Responding to Kate's attempts to reach him the last couple of weeks would only drag her down into his mess, so as much as he'd wanted her company, he'd chosen to distance himself.

He'd finally gotten his truck repaired, but that added another bill, not to mention that hike in his auto insurance rates.

Right now, he wanted to put those worries aside and enjoy a breather, this hour with Kate before he had to work at the Christmas tree lot tonight. He clicked off the ignition, music going silent. Houses outlining the bay reflected Christmas lights on the shimmering water.

She met him at the front door. "Hey, Zach. Welcome."

He glanced around for Haley.

"She's at work." She stepped back to give him room. "I'm glad you got my text."

He hung his coat on the clothes tree and then faced her, hyper aware of her scent and the fact he'd ignored the last few texts she and Haley had sent. "I'm sorry I've been out of reach. This stuff with Topher is challenging." He wouldn't get into his laundry list of problems.

"Please don't worry about it. We both understand and honestly, we're hurting for him, because he's obviously in pain."

Her words and her heart touched Zach. "Thanks."

"Think nothing of it. I know you're dealing with a lot."

One of those things was the accident. When Topher had asked about the damage, Zach had been careful to give only minimal details with the reassurance that Zach was fine. Toph seemed to let it go then. With the truck repaired, there wasn't a visual reminder anymore. That helped. He wondered if Kate's car was also fixed, but he wouldn't ask. He'd honor their decision to leave it behind them.

He followed her to the great room. She looked comfortable in her long, blue sweater over black leggings, complete with her adorable polar bear slippers. For some reason, that only made her more approachable and irresistible. He stifled a grunt at his own thoughts. No amount of caution could convince every part of him that Kate was off limits. His mind, and perhaps his heart, skittered in her wake.

"Hot cider, cocoa, or possibly coffee? Except, I don't know how to make it. I hate coffee and, thank goodness, so does Haley. Smells so awful." Her face scrunched, and he grinned. "But her parents have a fancy machine for their guests somewhere around here, if you wanna try."

With her, he could forget his worries. "Cider's fine. Thanks."

"Sure thing. My mom made this when I was growing up." She set a huge measuring cup on the granite, adding clear apple cider, pulp-free

OJ—just a splash—and two cinnamon sticks. "Now, a couple of minutes in the mic and we'll have something delicious to sip while we chat."

He propped himself against a nearby counter. "So, what's the latest with you?"

"I'm enjoying my time here."

He glanced around the great room. "Not too bad for a famous musician."

She scoffed playfully. "I do enjoy a bit of luxury, not gonna lie."

He laughed outright. What worries?

She pulled the full and steaming measuring cup from the microwave and then found two mugs. Using tongs, she fished out the cinnamon sticks, one for each cup. Next, she stirred the cider and poured it evenly into each mug. The scent of hot apples and cinnamon filled the room, a homey fragrance he'd missed.

She handed him his cup. "Here you go. Let's sit at the table. I'm terrified of spilling on their white furniture."

He agreed it seemed an odd choice for a rental, but he wouldn't judge.

Once she sat across from him, he tasted the cider. The perfect blend of flavors. "This is really good."

"Thanks." Her eyes sparkled.

He glanced toward the darkened windows and then back to the other side of the great room. "I enjoyed playing the piano. I'd love to live here, write music, forget the outside world for a while." He jolted, facing her again. "I hope that didn't sound like I think you're ignoring the real world."

"Oh, I didn't take it that way. No worries." She cupped her mug and, wearing a content expression, left things quiet between them.

Did she carry burdens right now too? Would it be prying to ask? He set his mug on a Christmas coaster. Better not to come across as interrogating. Seconds ticked by, and he'd need to leave soon. "You mentioned Topher in your text."

She met his eyes, sincerity shining in her personable gaze. "I want to be careful here. I'm pretty much a stranger to you, to him, and I don't want to cross any lines or alienate you."

He appreciated the consideration. "No worries," he echoed her earlier words. "I guess part of me feels like we know you, at least a little bit, through your music. It's as if we've gotten to see some of what's in your heart." Shoot that sounded corny. And intimate. He swallowed too-hot cider to hide his discomfort. *Stay on this side of those lines, dude.*

She breathed in the steam from her mug, not seeming to notice. "Or, I'm a really good actor."

Huh. He toyed with his coaster, spinning it on the table. "No . . ." He didn't believe that for a minute, not after meeting her. "I mean, I've put on a persona when I'm directing the choir at church, all social and cheerful. I've played recitals where I needed to be this happy guy pounding out fast-paced numbers. But I'm much more level than that, for the most part. For you, your originals have heart, depth, and you don't overplay them."

"Thank you. And let me say, that the *you* I've seen at the piano the last couple of times we've played seems like a sincere guy."

Her assessment touched him. He hadn't put on a façade with her, not after their uncomfortable first meeting. Why bother? She'd seen his failure that day. He trusted her. Was that why it felt like they'd known each other longer than a few weeks? "Thanks. And if you have any helpful input about Topher, please share it."

"Here's what I'm wondering—what if he

can't tell you what's wrong? I know you've asked him; I've watched you. But what if he doesn't know, and he gets frustrated, and that's when he lashes out? That would annoy me."

"Hmm. You may be right. I chatted with the counselor at his school and we never got that far, but it feels true." Zach's experience in counseling for himself had proven that when ideas clicked, they were usually a point to remember.

"He may need a psychologist to help him put his feelings into words."

Exactly what the school counselor said. She'd promised to reconnect with contact information for a few local child psychologists.

"He seems better the last couple of weeks, in some ways." Zach finished his cooling cider. "But I know it's not over. I appreciate your input, though, truly. Thank you."

"Sure. I'm certain you'll find the right help, and soon he'll be feeling better and excited for Christmas."

Zach hoped so.

She hesitated again, as if unsure if she should speak her thoughts. He inclined his head, a silent invitation. After a breath, she asked, "Will he see his mom... over Christmas? I'm assuming you have custody, but perhaps you share him during the holidays?"

No wonder she'd hesitated. Zach hadn't worn a ring for about two years, so Kate probably guessed he was divorced. This conversation just got harder. He inhaled deep. "His mother died in a car accident three years ago."

Kate went pale. "Oh, no," her words came out unsteadily, and she shot out of her chair. Her hands shook as she lifted her mug and carried it to the farthest sink.

Worried, he stood. "You okay? I know we talked about not mentioning our accident, but this is completely different." Surely she could see that.

Kate didn't answer. Instead she washed her hands, as if giving herself time to think.

Most people didn't respond like she had. Her change of demeanor. She acted . . . guilty? But that didn't make sense. Zach knew the killer's name, vehicle, all the grizzly details. None of them related to Kate. His gut tightening, he followed her. "Topher and I are doing all right. No need to worry about us."

"I-I'm fine. I just need to—will you excuse

me?" She darted down the hall toward the half bath near the entryway.

"Of course," he said, but she was already locked in.

Checking the time, he reran their conversation through his mind. She'd been okay, helpful even, making suggestions. And then suddenly, mention of Hannah's car accident had undone her.

Wait. She'd admitted a dislike of foggy night driving. She'd tailgated him as far as he'd let her to Birch Harbor on the dark highway.

Had Kate been in an earlier car accident too? He knew the nightmares, the anger, the helplessness. Thank God, literally, that Topher hadn't been in that car with his mom or learned any of the horrifying details.

Zach gave Kate a few minutes, never heard any running water, or any sound really. Finally, he padded down the hallway and tapped on the door with a knuckle. "You okay?" He held his breath, listening.

When she opened the door, her face was still pale.

"You all right?" he asked again, reaching toward her elbow in case she fainted.

She wouldn't meet his eyes. "I-I'll be fine. Sorry about that."

"Do you need a snack? Is it a blood sugar thing?" Hannah, his late wife, used to have strange symptoms if she hadn't eaten for several hours, and it was getting closer to dinner. Except, they'd just had cider.

"I'll try eating. S-sorry about this." Kate strode toward the kitchen. She didn't seem as shaky, but he kept up just in case he needed to catch her. Once again, she tugged on the protective side of him, a side he'd mostly exercised for his son in the last couple of years. At the fridge, she pulled out a small imported cheese circle and unwrapped it. "Want one?"

"I'm fine. Thank you. Let's sit. Can I grab some crackers for you too? Point me in that direction. Or maybe a banana? Glass of water?" He needed to leave in the next few minutes, but he couldn't walk away and wonder if she'd passed out behind him.

She indicated the pantry door and he found entertainment crackers, which he brought to the breakfast bar where she'd perched herself. After pouring a glass of ice water, he joined her on his own barstool. Was it best to be direct? Or would that further upset her? He'd begin with an apology. "I'm sorry that bringing up my late wife made you feel uncomfortable."

Her head shaking, she swallowed. "It's not that. I promise. Thank you for confiding in me. I'm so sorry for your loss..." She sipped the water and then munched on the cheese and crackers. He was glad to see her getting some calories, despite her obvious distress.

He waited for her to share more. If he let it, anger rose inside whenever he thought about the night of Hannah's accident. But Kate seemed unsettled. It'd be better to change the subject. "Let's switch gears."

"Okay . . . ," she said, grabbing another cracker. "You mentioned wanting to bring something up. It's your turn." She nodded toward him in a go-ahead gesture, the color in her face returning and her posture straighter.

"Let me make a quick call. I've got a shift in a few minutes down at Garrison's farm."

"Oh, shoot. I can let you go."

Still unsure if she was okay, he hesitated. But Clay had given him this job, and Zach didn't want to let him down. "Are you positive?"

"Of course." She stood. "I'll walk you to the

door." She seemed strong, so he moved in that direction. "Listen, I wanted to pitch an idea to you. Would you be interested in writing music with me?"

He froze, shoe half on. "Absolutely."

"Well, that was easy."

"And would you be interested in putting together a number for the church program—perhaps a duet? I know it's not a paid gig and you're a star, but I'd love if you could be part of the concert." He grinned up at her from the bench.

She swatted the air near him for his playful words. She wasn't a star. "I'd be happy to. A quid pro quo."

"Perfect." He stood, shoving his arms into his jacket sleeves. "I'll be in touch." He reached for her elbow. "You're sure you're okay?"

"Yup. Thanks. See you later." She held the door open, and he passed through. "Take care. I hope Topher feels better soon."

Thirteen

Rain drenched the December afternoon, gushing off rooftops and pounding the waterside deck. Whitecaps dotted the bay, and winds threw water against the house. Kate stood at the living room's large windows, clutching a mug of hot peach tea, watching the storm.

Her phone rang. Caller ID read HEATH. *Ugh.* She didn't answer, but instead set her phone on the nearest table. As far as she was concerned, they'd covered every necessary issue. The man only wanted attention, or a chance to see how her writing was coming. The ringing started again after a short pause. He wasn't going to stop calling until they talked.

"Hello, Heath," she answered, guards going

up. "What is so urgent?"

"I'm having a hard time writing without you around," he said, his voice sounding more nasally than she remembered. "Are you still on Whidbey?"

She could guess where this was going. He'd slant his argument to make her look incompetent, all while adopting a condescending tone full of shame and blame. Her best bet? Maintain a strong boundary. And seriously, how had his shortcomings never bothered her before?

"Don't even think about finding me, Heath. We are *not* writing together. Those days are over. Finish what you can. I'll do the same. *Then* we'll get together as a group, during reasonable hours, and work out any kinks as planned."

His sigh whistled through the phone. "For the sake of the band, I think we need to overlook our personality conflicts, be *adult* about this, and get these new songs ready." His scare tactics had risen to a new level. Heath wasn't the same guy he'd been a few months ago.

"You are not going to bully me into seeing you. Back off."

"Fine. But if the next album bombs because

you can no longer be a team player, that's on you." He clicked off the call.

Kate gripped her phone tight and considered throwing it against the farthest wall. Worse than his manipulation was the fact that her own creativity had dried up. Not a single song since she'd come to the island, even here, with this bayside view. And since when did she *need* a cowriter?

Zach's face came to mind. He'd agreed to write with her, but they hadn't scheduled anything. How were things going with Topher? She would try reaching him again, check on him, and schedule writing time. Next visit, they'd avoid the topic of car accidents.

Had she really lost all composure when Zach learned she was a negligent and now-dependent driver who'd failed miserably one foggy night? Could she just take back that conversation? Especially after discovering that's how Topher's mom had died. Rehashing it all wasn't helping her. She couldn't blame Zach for his anger and possible unforgiveness around the crash that claimed his wife. How awful.

Shaking free of those thoughts, she dialed his number before she could talk herself out of it. He answered ahead of the second ring. "Hi, Kate."

Shoot, she loved hearing his voice on the phone. Yum. *Stop it!* If anything should confirm her dating break, it was that conversation with Heath minutes ago. "Hey. Is this a good time?"

"Sure. On my way back to the church to drop off supplies for Saturday's rehearsal."

"About that, do you still want a cellist?"

"Let me see," he began, his voice teasing. "Yes, but only if she's a professional who doesn't mind entertaining families for free at Christmas. Someone who can pull something together rather quickly now that it's December. Know anybody like that?"

"Well, when you put it that way..."

"Seriously, I think you'll be the hit of the night." She heard the smile in his voice. She pictured him driving his truck wearing plaid flannel and his sherpa-lined leather coat over jeans and boots, a relaxed hand draped on the wheel.

"I think the kids will be, but okay." Her smile spread despite herself.

"Well, they may . . ." His truck motor went quiet as if he'd shut off the engine.

"I have a request though."

"Oh, yeah?" The playful challenge in his voice sent a hitch into her throat.

"Yeah. I need two things, actually." She loved bantering with him.

"Heh. Okay. Shoot."

"One, you and Topher must come over for dinner some night before Saturday."

"Done."

She grinned. "Cool. Next, we need to schedule a writing session. I get that it's a busy season, but I'm desperate here." She'd already explained to him about her next album's timing. But lately, she'd reconsidered. She and Zach could release a single, without involving the group. Maybe it was time she branched out.

"I agreed to do it. I'm in. But we need to collaborate when Topher's happy with my sister. No more outbursts."

"I hope he's okay."

Zach's sigh came through the phone like a quiet breath in her ear. "We'll get there."

"I believe you will. And finally, what about your tree farm job? I don't want to keep you from immediate income in order to work on this with me. Not that we won't make money.

Eventually, we will—"

"Kate. Stop trying to talk me out of it. I'll figure out the rest."

"Okay. Then, yay!" Giddiness bubbled inside her. "When can we start?"

"After dinner Wednesday? Are you game?"

"Definitely."

Fourteen

The windshield wipers barely kept up with the December deluge as Zach pulled down Kate's driveway midweek. The whole way here, he'd mentally directed himself in acceptable professional interaction. After his doctor's news, he had more reason than before to keep things from getting too personal.

No matter how beautiful, caring, warm, and musical Kate was. No matter how much Topher looked up to her and how she doted on the kid. No matter that Zach and Topher both adored her and her music, Zach had to keep things friendly.

"I hate the rain," Topher said, his face a mask of sadness. Thankfully, he hadn't brought up his idea that Kate would make a good mom again. Had he forgotten? Zach hoped he didn't embarrass them both tonight.

"How come, buddy?" This month was notorious for darkness and downpours. Did the fall season bother his son? Not much Zach could do about that, short of moving to Arizona or Hawaii.

As was normal these days, Topher didn't respond. Did he hate this weather for the same reasons Zach did? He parked the truck and using the garage's outdoor lights to see, he followed Topher, who darted toward the front door and then stood under the protective roof.

Somewhere in the distance a dog barked. The humid, heavy air carried the scent of evergreens, but also the aroma of snow from the Olympic or Cascade Mountain ranges, and even a hint of salt from the harbor.

Cello music drifted through the closed door, solitary and strong. "Silent Night." Topher froze, eyes bright, his head cocked as he listened, not in any hurry to knock on the door and no trace of sadness. The music stopped, and Kate appeared in their line of sight through the windows, lit by the chandelier overhead, waving, cheerful. Beautiful. She wore a red sweater over black skinny jeans and those playful bear slippers.

"C'mon in, fellas," she said as she swung open the door. "Welcome." From her earlobes hung Christmas tree earrings that danced in the light.

The air smelled of vanilla, and a sense of home settled over Zach as it often did when he visited. Crazy. This wasn't even Kate's house. Maybe it wasn't the building, but rather the company.

It's a business arrangement.

Right. Zach sat on the short bench to remove his boots. "Thanks for having us." She probably had no idea, but their stopovers to see her, in this atmosphere, had brightened an otherwise dull, dark, lonely late autumn. He made eye contact. Maybe she'd read gratitude in his expression. Or he could find a time to tell her later. Except, he didn't want to give her the wrong idea. It'd be best if he could convince that longing-for-home feeling inside to *sub*side.

Not likely.

"We heard you playing. Didn't want to knock and make you stop." Toph dropped to the floor and yanked off his shoes.

"Well, that was considerate of you."

Standing once again, Topher faced Kate. Zach froze. His son fidgeted, hands making fists, but then releasing. "I'm sorry for breaking the ornament last time."

Zach breathed out his relief. They'd chatted about how Topher should apologize, but Zach hadn't expected him to do it the moment they walked in. Good for Toph.

Kate crouched down. "You know what, kiddo? You're brave to say that. Thank you. And I want you to know Miss Haley and I are not upset. You're forgiven." Her kind eyes smiled into Topher's face. And Zach's heart flipped.

The kid seemed ready to bolt for the living area. "Okay."

Standing, with pride swelling in his chest, Zach clapped Topher's shoulder and gave him a nod his son would surely understand. *Well done.* Then, Zach peered around. "Is Haley coming?" She'd provide a helpful buffer.

"Not tonight. She's gotta work." Kate pointed toward the living area. "C'mon in."

"Wait. Dad?"

"Yeah?"

"Did you say you and Miss Kate are going to

do a song for church that night the kids' choir sings?"

He hated to trigger his son, but since he couldn't be sure what set him off, Zach would answer questions until Topher gave a signal. "That's right."

"I wanna play with you two."

Zach exchanged glances with Kate, who wore a relaxed smile. Then, he focused back on his son. "What did you have in mind?"

"I don't know. What song are you doing?"

They hadn't yet made that decision.

"I have a suggestion," Kate said, speaking slowly, palms facing out. "What if we did 'Carol of the Bells' and you played bells with us?"

Zach studied Topher's face. Of course, that'd be a new arrangement—less classy and more casual. "Jingle Bells" might be a better song choice. Unless Toph could control how often he shook them.

"I like it!" The kiddo seemed confident now, but come showtime, would he choke? If he broke down tonight, Zach would cancel their practice. He hadn't come expecting to rehearse for the program, but he also hadn't seen Topher this excited about anything lately.

"Are you sure, Son? In front of an audience?" Of course, at the last minute he and Kate could just perform without Topher. They'd keep their new arrangement simple, but they could each improvise a more intricate version if needed.

"Sounds fine to me," Kate said, "if it's okay with your dad."

His son faced him. "Please?"

"We can try it. I'm glad you want to join us, Toph." To Kate he said, "He has a good sense of rhythm." That reminded Zach he wanted to buy a starter drum kit for him for Christmas. Still needed to get on that. If he could afford it. They'd put the set in the basement of the rental house, near the upright piano.

Kate caught his eye, her brows raised as if checking in. After all, they'd discussed not doing music with Topher in the house to avoid further outbursts. *This okay?*

Zach nodded. So often lately, he took his cues from Toph. But Zach would be sure he was positioned where he could study his son's face. The first sign of tears, they'd redirect.

She hefted her cello from its stand. "Shall we, gentlemen?"

"Just like a family," Topher said under his

breath, and Zach wondered if he'd heard him correctly as he settled at the piano. "Wait! I don't have any bells."

"Of course!" Kate set aside her cello once more. "I saw a box of toys in the storage closet under the stairs. Maybe there are instruments." She disappeared and moments later returned with wooden-handled sleigh bells, which she passed to Topher in a noisy exchange. "This was all I could find. Maybe we could figure something else out later?"

Sleigh bells wouldn't complicate their performance at all. Predictably, Topher shook the multi-belled noisemaker to a deafening crescendo, and Zach let him go on for several seconds. Finally, Kate grimaced. Time for a rescue. "Son, listen." Zach waited for him to hold the toy still. Once the sounds died down, Zach said, "We'll have to decide when the best times are for you to chime in." Kate chuckled at his pun, and Zach grinned. "Okay?" First chance he had, he'd replace that contraption with a single bell and coach his kiddo in how to handle it.

"Sure, Dad." Such ready compliance. Topher kept glancing between the two adults. Was he adding things together and forming a new family?

"What if I played a staccato opening, and Topher played a light jingle in rhythm along with me?" Kate reached for her bow. "Then, you could come in with the melody on the piano. That's when I'll play legato. We'll bring Topher back in at about two-thirds and then at the end for a grand finish. Thoughts?"

"Let's do it!" Excited, Topher started to raise his arms in the air, and the bells went off. He stilled them. "Oops." He gave a playful grin, and Zach smiled back.

"Good catch." Their playing together could be a hit with the families in the audience, if it worked.

After a few false starts, Topher caught on quickly and cooperated better than Zach had expected. Perhaps keeping the kiddo out of the music wasn't the answer. Maybe he'd only wanted to be involved.

A half hour later, they'd decided on an arrangement and made it through the piece twice. After setting her cello in its stand, Kate high-fived a beaming Topher.

Zach stood from the piano bench. His brother-in-law would arrive in the next forty-five minutes to pick up Topher so the adults could focus on songwriting. "We'd better work on dinner."

Topher talked nonstop about the excitement of being included. They sat down to mac and cheese and chicken fingers, which Zach guessed Kate had tailored directly for his son. They were nearly through the first phase of the evening. So far, nothing embarrassing—or worse, alarming—had happened.

Kate forked a bite of steamed asparagus, watching Topher. The boy stared off toward the living room and around at the kitchen. "Dad, we should move here. I mean, it's beautiful. And Kate lives here."

So much for an uneventful evening. "I like this house too," Zach said, offering an apologetic expression in Kate's direction. "But we have a home."

Kate leaned toward Topher. "Plus, did you know I don't own this house? I'm only renting it."

"Oh." Topher's expression fell and so did his gaze.

"Your uncle will be here in about five minutes, and then you can go play with your cousins. Let's wash up and get your shoes and coat on." Zach held his breath, anticipating a battle. But Topher hopped up and silently carried his plate to the sink.

After he'd washed his hands, he returned to the table. "Thank you for letting me be part of the music."

Kate seemed to melt. "My pleasure, Topher. We'll have fun at the Christmas program."

"I wish I could be part of your family."

Kate's surprised expression matched Zach's gut punch. "Hey, Toph, let's get those shoes on."

Topher dragged himself to the bench by the front door. Behind him, Zach and Kate exchanged shrugs and unspoken questions. Why did his son talk like this at Kate's and then never speak of it again?

"Kate, could I have a minute with Topher?"

"Absolutely. I've got to tidy up that kitchen." She kept her voice upbeat and her posture energetic. "I'll see you later, okay, kiddo?" She reached to give him a side hug, and he obliged in a sweet moment of closing his eyes and wearing a sad smile. Zach had to look away.

"Bye, Miss Kate."

As soon as she'd skittered down the hall, Zach whispered, "Buddy, I can tell you care about Miss Kate. But what was that about? Why did you mention being part of Kate's family?"

"Because she'd make a good mommy. I already told you." He shoved his arms in his coat, not bothering to keep his voice as quiet as Zach had. "And I'm not afraid to tell her that—unlike you. I like her. And that's that."

Was Zach afraid? Was that the battle inside? No. What did a seven-year-old boy know of grownup relationships? Zach hadn't known much at that age himself. "Listen. First, Miss Kate doesn't live here permanently. Second, she's got a busy career, traveling all over the place for work. I can't travel like that. And neither can you."

"But none of that matters, Dad, if you like her." His direct gaze unnerved Zach. "Right?"

A horn honked outside—their time was up. He'd slipped his shoes and jacket on too, partly to use his nervous energy. Zach put a hand on his son's shoulder for the walk to the dark driveway. "I'm really proud of you. You played well tonight, and everyone had a good time."

"I loved it!"

"Good. I like watching you enjoy music with

me."

"With all three of us, Dad. All three of us. Like a family."

Adam had climbed from his family's SUV and stood at the open rear passenger door. "I cleared a space of your cousins' mess just for you, bud."

Zach verified the seat belt fit snugly and was about to close the door when Topher stopped him. "Think about it, Dad. Just think about it."

"Right." He gave Adam a look. No doubt his brother-in-law, nephews and nieces, and his sister were about to get an earful of Topher's new family plan. Perfect. "I'll see you in a couple of hours."

"Bye."

Zach sighed into the cold, damp night after they'd backed out and he waved into the darkness. Yeah. Family. Sure.

He slipped into the warm house and found Kate in the living room, cello in place, posture board straight. "Sorry about that."

She met his eyes. "Everything okay?"

"You know how kids are," he said, taking his spot at the piano. "I tried to explain to him about your work and how much you travel, but

I'm not sure he gets it."

She nodded, which Zach took to mean they agreed. The adults understood why the seven-year-old's fantasy wouldn't work.

"He really likes you, and I can't blame him." The air went still and Zach jolted, meeting her eyes. Why had he said that? "Sorry, now *I'm* making things uncomfortable."

"Relax, okay? I'm just concerned about him." Her kind, welcoming expression shouldn't surprise him anymore. No wonder Topher was drawn to her. Zach felt an urge to lean in himself. "And I'm here for both of you."

"Thanks." His son's words echoed in his head, especially, *I'm not afraid.*

Well, Zach couldn't say the same.

Fifteen

S it and spill," Lacy demanded that night when Zach arrived to pick up his son, later than he'd planned. "I've got time and since the kids all fell asleep in the den an hour ago, you do too."

Hands jammed in his jacket pockets, Zach searched the kitchen and dining area for any sign of his brother-in-law.

Lacy caught him. "Adam won't save you."

Zach groaned and climbed onto the nearest barstool. "Fine." Might as well face this head on. "I'm guessing you got an earful."

Perched on her own stool, Lacy ticked items off on her fingers. "Your son's joining you and Miss Famous One for a Christmas trio at church."

Miss Famous One?

Another finger stood with the first. "He sees you three as a possible family because, and I quote, 'She's beautiful, Aunt Lacy. And Dad loves her, he just won't say it. She would make a great mom.'"

Zach scrubbed a hand down his face, a low rumble vibrating in his chest as he moaned.

"And then, and this is the scariest part." She kept her voice low while humor faded from her face.

Zach raised his head, met her familiar brown eyes.

"You still haven't told me what your doctor said. Not that your son mentioned that, of course."

Zach didn't know where to start. How much to divulge. As her older brother, he'd always had a trusting relationship with Lacy, but she did sometimes meddle, if he let her get too far into his world.

"Plus," she added, wearing a smirk, "what happened to nine o'clock? It's ten thirty."

He'd lost track of time, filling Kate's mansion with music. They'd cowritten a promising song—just a duet, though her guitarist and vocalist could certainly add to the piano and cello parts if Kate chose to pitch it to Prism Effect. He still couldn't believe he'd gotten this chance to participate in his favorite ensemble's music, gotten this close to Kate.

He returned to the moment, and Lacy simply grinned at him. "I can see from that dopey expression we're going to need cocoa. So while you figure out what to say next, I'll hop to it."

She boiled up her homemade hot chocolate and settled back at the breakfast bar next to him with two mugs, whipped cream, and mini-marshmallows within reach. "Your son seemed more animated tonight than usual. Is he doing better? Or was that an auntie's wishful thinking?"

His kiddo seemed a safe topic. Zach was grateful Lacy had decided to begin with Toph, without using his name in case he walked in. For a few moments, Zach could deflect from himself and his confusing thoughts about Miss Famous One.

"He's a mystery. He cries when we play music—he doesn't cry when we play music. He won't talk to me; he will talk to Kate. He's angry. He's sad. He's excited. I figured he'd want to avoid the Christmas program. Instead, he wants to be right up there on stage with Kate and me, performing." Zach took a moment to drop a handful of minimarshmallows into his drink. They bounced and came up coated in chocolate.

"His school counselor put me in touch with a child psychologist who can't fit us in just yet. Meanwhile, my doctor in Mukilteo wants a bigger piece of me—getting the surrounding area to see if there are any more anomalies." Zach wouldn't entertain the idea of melanoma. If his doc didn't name it, yet, he wouldn't either.

"Is she worried?"

"Cautious—her word."

Lacy sipped her doctored cocoa, whipped cream tamed by her spoon. "Are *you* worried?"

Hands around his still-full, hot mug, he met her eyes again. "For his sake"—he nodded toward the den—"you betcha."

"You know Adam and I will do everything we can to help."

Zach's throat went tight. "He's already lost his mom."

Lacy reached for Zach and covered his wrist with her warm hand. "I know. But he's got us." She squeezed. "All of us."

She gave him a minute as he gulped his drink. Finally, she said, "So, you and Miss Famous One?"

Zach met Lacy's eyes, suddenly beyond tired. "I can't." He almost started ticking off his own list, but he lacked the energy for playfulness so he left his hands around the mug. "Feels unfaithful to Hannah. I might be in for the fight of my life. My son is mysteriously moody." He wouldn't mention his financial stress.

"Your son seems to really like her."

"I don't doubt it." He drained half his mug. "I can't blame him."

"Hey, any chance God's in this?"

Hard to picture that lately, especially when Zach feared leaving his child an orphan. He pressed his lips together, considering his escape plan.

"Keep an open mind, okay? Don't let fear shut down what God starts up."

He stood and offered her a hug. His paraphrase of that verse returned to him—*Cast your cares on God because He cares for you.*

Lacy released him. "Let's go get your sleepy boy."

"I think you should tell him how you feel." December fifth, before Haley's shift, the best friends strung exterior Christmas lights in the afternoon drizzle.

"Who, Heath?"

"Uh, no. You know who I mean."

Kate pushed back her hood with a wet sleeve, smearing water over her forehead. "This is loads of fun in the rain."

Haley unwound the wrapped string and handed up the next section to Kate on the small ladder. "Deflecting."

"Yup." These clear lights would brighten this porch on winter's short days.

"Topher likes you."

"Yup." She tucked the wires around a hook. The wind blew mist at her sideways, and she shivered. Haley probably had a point, but Kate had promised herself she wouldn't entertain the idea of a relationship with another pianist. Then, Kate had made the mistake of cowriting with him and telling Haley all the details. The magic of their session.

"He's not Heath."

"I know." After climbing down, Kate shifted the ladder to the next section. Almost finished.

Haley went still, the light strands wrapped around her arm. "I get that you're scared. Perfectly natural."

Was it fear? Or wisdom? "I don't see it that way."

Haley only nodded then left things quiet for a moment.

"Maybe it's time for a heart-to-heart with him." Haley released more slack, and Kate went back to work. "Given all your chemistry together, I'm guessing he feels the same way. But you won't know until you talk about it."

"He's a widower. He's probably afraid too."

"I agree, and you just gave yourself away." Haley handed up the last of the strand. "That will do it. Let's go warm up."

Fine. So, Kate was afraid. Zach had similarities with Heath, several of them. She didn't want to repeat her mistakes. Who could blame her for that?

Sixteen

Thanks for coming over, Zach." They'd planned to finish their composition today after church. But first, Kate had a few things to say. "I think we should clear the air."

The lit gas fireplace set a romantic mood on this gloomy afternoon, but Kate positioned them at the dining table. Last night's rehearsal at church had been awkward between them, Topher declaring to the room of musicians waiting their turn to rehearse on the stage that Kate would one day be his new mommy. Zach's face had gone red as he rushed to quiet his son.

After hearing Topher declare he'd like to live with Kate, she hadn't been completely surprised by his words. Had Zach?

"I know it's your only afternoon off following a full morning at church."

"No problem." Across the table, Zach fidgeted. He'd refused even a beverage, but now he seemed uncomfortable as if unsure what to do with his hands. "Actually, could we have ice water? I don't mind getting it." He was already on his feet.

"Sure." She stayed in her seat. Yeah, this heart-to-heart had started off well.

He returned to the table with two glasses and set one on the coaster in front of her. "I need to apologize for my son's words at rehearsal."

Which meant Zach didn't feel anything romantic toward Kate. Right? Or perhaps she inferred too much. And why was that both disappointing and a relief at once? "Don't worry about it."

"I mean, I know you're only here for the season. Toph can't understand that." Zach chugged water, ice cubes clinking loudly in the quiet room.

"Well, as long as we're apologizing. I want to say I'm sorry for your loss."

He gave her a warm nod.

"And I'm sorry for wigging out when we discussed car accidents."

Finally, Zach sat. He wore a mask of concern. "Sounds like it still haunts you. The fog and whatever happened that day." A chagrinned expression covered his face. "And then, I crashed into you on your first night here."

"You know, oddly that accident wasn't a big deal. I've got my wagon back, fixed. I'm okay with leaving that out of this. Is your truck going to be okay?"

"Yes. Good as new."

"Back to what you said about my earlier accident haunting me. It does, but I'll get a handle on it." She ran her fingers over the light condensation on her glass. "Honestly, I was more embarrassed than anything else. For you to see me that way."

"I like seeing the various sides of you. Plus, we all have tough spots in our pasts. I sure do."

His guards coming down gave her courage. She'd use a gentle voice. "Is missing his mom what's eating Topher?"

Zach rested his elbows on the table and leaned in. "She died when he was four, so I'm sometimes unsure how much he remembers her. He says he doesn't have a lot of memories."

"It does sound like he's ready to move forward."

Zach grunted, leaned back, and drained his glass. "Thus, his insistence you'd be a great mom for him." A sheepish smile followed.

Hearing Zach say it himself hit Kate in a way that she hadn't expected—like an unintentional invitation, or maybe a threat. "I need to tell you about Heath."

Brow furrowing, Zach met her eyes. "He's the pianist in Prism Effect, right?"

"Yes. We dated for a few years. And we got engaged a while ago."

"Wait. You're engaged?" His attention darted to her ringless left hand.

"No. Not anymore."

"Oh. That's too bad." The sentence came out more of a question.

"It's for the best, believe me. I should have listened to Hales."

Zach pressed his lips together as if debating where to go next. Finally, he said, "So, you're not together anymore. Is there a chance of your getting back with him?"

"Ha. I hope not."

"You sound like breaking up with him bothers you less than that car accident, if you don't mind me saying so."

She mock toasted his words with a tipped glass in midair. "You got it. But, I promised myself not to date another musician, especially one I work closely with."

Zach waited a few moments before speaking. "My feelings aside, I would think you'd have a lot in common with a fellow musician. What? Would you prefer a botanist or a lamp designer?"

She chuckled. "Random."

He shrugged a strong shoulder, the atmosphere lightening around them.

"Botanist, definitely."

He laughed aloud this time.

She loved the sound, and she wasn't going to let him off the hook. At last, they were getting down to her agenda for their chat. "You mentioned your feelings. Let's talk about that."

He licked his lips, but he met her eyes. "'Kay."

She'd hide a little bit here. "Haley insists you and I have chemistry."

"Haley's right."

She swallowed. Now what?

"After Topher filled my sister in on *ev-ery-thing* the other night—according to a seven-year-old—Lacy confronted me with, 'Don't let fear shut down what God starts up.'" Those words floated in the cinnamon candle-scented air between them.

Was that what she was doing? She'd been burned.

"I like making music with you." No sign of squirming now.

Couldn't argue with that. "Same," she said.

"But that means we keep working closely together and that means..." He let his words trail off. Moments later, he broke eye contact.

"You're disqualified," she supplied, rethinking her rules.

"Except, there's something I haven't told you yet."

She rather liked them delving into all this transparency. Refreshing. And for now, she didn't feel afraid. "What's that?"

"I'm facing a health situation."

"Oh, no. On top of everything else?"

"It's nothing so far. But my doc is watching it closely."

Evening pushed in, darkening the room. To

give Zach space, Kate stood and flipped on a few lamps around the living area. Would he mind sharing his diagnosis, or whatever, with her?

When she sat, he met her eyes again. "I don't want to date right now—not with all these complications. Wouldn't be fair."

"Understood." She sighed, part of her relieved. A bigger part of her conflicted. "I'm sorry to hear of your health problem. I'll pray for you."

"Thank you."

"If you'd rather not finish working on our song tonight, I completely understand."

"No, that's fine. The upcoming couple of weeks will be busy with the church program."

"And Christmas."

"Right. Speaking of, Lacy wanted me to invite you over to her house. It's loud and crazy and overwhelming, but we'd love to have you join us. Unless you're with Haley's family."

"Her parents are out of state, so yeah, she and I were going to hang out. You and Topher are welcome to drop by here if you'd like though, maybe in the afternoon?"

"Thanks. We'll see." Zach stood, pointing toward the piano. "Shall we?"

"Absolutely." Good. Things were settled. No relationship. No dating. No risk. Only a close working arrangement with her peering over his shoulder while he scrawled music notes on the staff paper, his pine scent wafting up to woo her.

This was good. A wise setup. Someone should convince her heart of that, especially after he'd mentioned his feelings but had never stated what they were.

Zach had hoped they could talk things out, discuss how each felt. List their objections. And they had. So, why the weighty disappointment? They'd made a wise choice, forgoing a relationship. They'd protected Topher, though the kiddo wouldn't understand. Zach's future was uncertain. Kate was a traveling musician without a true home right now. After Christmas she'd head to King or Kitsap County or wherever and record Prism Effect's next album before their tour began, taking her around the world.

Zach focused on savoring each moment of

Christmas lights, the aroma of cinnamon, flames in the fireplace flickering while Kate played her cello, her eyes bright. They finished their new composition and chatted about recording the piece as a duet.

As he slipped his coat on to leave, she stood waiting in the entryway. She wore an uncertain expression, mirroring his own questions. "There's a new, small sound studio in Birch Harbor. Do you think we should wait until January to record? It'll be tight next year for me, but less inconvenient for you."

"I can get several hours off if I have notice. So, let's record this month, as busy as it is." He couldn't promise anything come January.

"We need a name for the piece," she said. "It's a Christmas song, so let's find something seasonal."

"Okay, um. How about we mention garland or holly or something?" His gaze traveled the room, coming to rest on the chandelier. "You know, I'm kinda surprised Haley hasn't hung mistletoe in here, trying to trick us."

Kate gestured toward the door frame behind him. "Me too!"

His thoughts went to places off limits, so he refocused on the discussion. "Mistletoe would make a good song title."

"I like it." She shuffled her feet. Did she feel as unwilling for him to leave as he did? "I am sorry about your medical scare."

Fighting the urge to take her hand, he shoved his fists into his jacket pockets. "Thanks. And for the record, Kevin or Keith or Heathcliff is a dolt."

"Ha! Well, Hales and I agree, so..."

Her grin lit up her face, and he couldn't help it. He stepped closer, reaching for her forearm and sliding his hand toward hers. Her eyebrows hiked with surprise, but she twined her fingers with his. "Tonight was fun," he murmured, his voice weakened by awareness.

"It was."

Chemistry. She'd used the word and that zing surrounded them now as she blinked up at him, standing closer than she'd done before. Christmas lights sent glimmers into the room from the front porch, making her golden-brown hair glisten. Loneliness overwhelmed him. Maybe his son had a point. "Do you think Topher's right?"

"What?" Her word barely emerged.

"He has no problem saying that he cares about you." Fear still held Zach back.

"I care about him too."

The waves of her hair over her shoulder drew his fingers, and he reached up to see if it was as soft as it looked. It was. "Is fear keeping us from seeing what others see?"

As if involuntarily, she closed her eyes, leaning into his hand at her ear. That about undid his resolve. They hadn't solved any of their challenges, and he wouldn't put Kate through the stress of whatever was next for him. He stepped back, his hand falling to his side. "Good night," he murmured.

She released his other hand, a touch of hurt in her eyes. "'Night."

"If things were different..."

Nodding, she said, "I get it. I really do." Still, she wore pain in her eyes, like rejection or doubt.

But he couldn't fix that. He'd done all he could. So, he offered one last tender smile and quietly slipped outside into the chilly evening.

Seventeen

Using spare moments, Kate and Zach polished their duet. Zach suggested they perform it as the finale for the program at church. Today, they'd go into the studio. Lacy had Topher, and Zach's pastor had let him off for several hours. He and Kate had agreed to meet at a local studio, which was in a building one block behind the Garrison's flower shop, Seaside Floral, in Birch Harbor.

"Hey, Zach," Kate said, reaching into the back of her station wagon for her cello case.

He held the door for her and then followed her inside.

Before long, the crew directed them to set up in Studio C at the back of the building. Kate had brought her favorite producer into town—

Jon Porter. He had a lot of experience, and Zach could appreciate that.

"We'll have creative control," she'd told Zach. "And we have five hours, though we may not need that much time."

Zach hadn't worked in a studio very often, certainly not since college, but the setup and work felt natural. He settled at the baby grand piano, warming up with scales and chords.

Kate knew of an almost immediate way of getting today's creation out to sales outlets. But first, they must lay down a solid version of the song. He needed to bring his best effort. No distractions.

Except, this morning, his son's school counselor would sit in on a meeting between Topher and a child psychologist to try to reach a diagnosis. They had agreed Zach shouldn't be present, hoping the seven-year-old would relax. Cathy had promised to call after the appointment to either give Zach the news or schedule a parent meeting.

"You okay?" Kate finished setting up in the space across from him. They would easily be able to see each other.

He shook off his thoughts. "Yeah, I'm good."

"Is Topher's meeting today? He told me about it."

Zach grunted. "He did?"

"Yeah. I'm sorry you can't be there."

"Oh, no. They said it would be too distracting for Toph. I get that. I just worry about him, you know? But I'm going to set all that aside so we can work on this. You have my full attention."

"Okay, guys. Whenever you're ready." Jon gave them a nod from the booth. Zach hoped they could recreate the magic of the other night, and though she didn't say it, perhaps Kate hoped for that too.

"Oh, one more thing," Jon said. "I need a song title."

"'Mistletoe,'" Kate said, reminding Zach of their moment as he left the other night. *Focus.*

"Great. 'Mistletoe' it is. Take one."

Kate counted them off and then played the intro they'd agreed on. She was the consummate professional. With a concentrated effort, Zach kept up, surprising himself.

"Great work," Jon said from the booth after the last notes had fully faded.

"Let's hear it back," Kate said as she set her cello in a nearby stand.

Zach's phone buzzed in his pocket, and he pulled it out. "I'm sorry, I have to take this call. Feel free to listen while I'm gone."

He stepped outside the building and answered, keeping his voice low. These studios were soundproof, but he'd still be considerate. "This is Zach." He stood under the overhang at the back door.

"Hi, Zach. This is Cathy at Topher's school. I have news for you. Any chance you can swing by my office before we lock up at three thirty today?"

He did some mental math. "That might be tight. Could you tell me on the phone?"

"No, sorry. I think it would be better to chat in person so I can give you some resources."

His gut sank. "Which means the psychologist found something specific."

"Yes."

Zach waited, but Cathy didn't say anything else. Neck tight, he rolled his shoulders. "Okay. I'll be there as soon as I can."

"Thank you."

"Bye." He clicked off and dropped his head. He'd tried his "cast your cares on God" nudge a few nights ago. And he had found peace for a bit. But heaviness settled on him again in the wake of Cathy's call. Amidst all the pressure of the moment, he'd forgotten to ask how Topher was doing. Maybe he should call back. See, a mother would think like that—*how is he now? Does he seem okay?* Those thoughts didn't occur to Zach until after the call was disconnected. But all he could do was try. So, he'd keep supporting his son. Whatever resources Cathy had in mind, he'd seriously consider them.

They finally had a possible answer. Maybe Zach's reaction should be hope instead of dread.

He stepped back into the studio to keep his commitment for the next hour or two. The song playback hit the final measures when he closed the door. Kate stood in the booth with Jon, pointing at the faders, making comments Zach couldn't hear through the glass.

"Everything okay?" Kate asked into the booth's mic.

Zach nodded. It would be.

Kate didn't seem convinced, but she let it go. "Ok, we'll start it over. It sounds pretty good."

Since he wasn't holding a mic, he gave her a thumbs-up. Jon hit a button, and their music filled the room. Pushing his worries aside, Zach focused in on each note. This was when they'd decide what needed work and whether they'd do more takes together or change the plan and record their tracks separately.

Closing his eyes, he lost himself in the music. Soon, a sense of . . . what? Joy or excitement built in him. He'd felt something the other day playing it with her, even while cowriting, and this confirmed it. Their Christmas duet was magical.

The song ended, and he found himself grinning.

A click sounded and then Jon's voice. "Join us, Zach?"

He stepped into the booth. "Hey." He met Kate's eyes, which now reminded him of ice on a wintry morning reflecting the sky. But if she had ice-blue eyes, they were the warmest in the state.

She raised her eyebrows. "Thoughts?"

"It's difficult to be objective, but I loved it. What did you two think?"

Kate wore her professional face. "Jon, could you cue up the bridge?"

Jon worked the mouse and soon music played through the studio.

"This part. Where the piano—"

A note Zach hadn't noticed struck him as discordant. He made a face. Obviously, he was more distracted than he'd guessed. "I missed that."

"And this." Kate extended her index finger, following the melody through the air until another bad note rang. Had Zach really messed up that often? Clearly, he wasn't touring performer material.

"No problem, we can fix it," Jon said. "I can either pitch correct them here, or you can replay them. Then, we put it together."

"Cool. Let's go again." A second chance to prove himself.

Kate didn't seem annoyed, but something had changed in her demeanor. If only he could ask her about it. But not now, not here.

Did Zach know how much this meant to her? A couple of bad notes did not detract from the amazing creativity they had together. And that was making her rethink her entire future. At this moment, as she repositioned herself with her cello while Zach took his position at the piano, she couldn't see herself ever playing music with Heath again. Period.

Would anybody mind if she only made music with Zach from now on? She suppressed a grin and gave him a nod. The poor guy seemed anxious. The first two retakes resulted in other mistakes, and soon she decided to call a time-out. "Hey, Jon, could we have a minute?"

"I'll take five." Jon stepped out of the booth.

Kate put her cello aside. "Hey, Zach, what's happening?"

He checked his phone, stood, and moved away from the piano. She joined him a few feet from the bench. "I guess I got a little wigged out, hearing those mistakes I don't remember making. I'll get it." He gave a hard nod, but it read as unsure.

"Listen, relax. You're among friends here. Jon is rooting for us. And you're excellent." She gave him a moment to absorb those words. Something distracted him this afternoon. Would he share it? "Is this about that call? How's your son?"

"He's okay. They have news for me. I need to head over to the school before three thirty."

"All right. Let me know if there's anything I

can do."

He gave her a warm smile. "You have been such a big help this whole time. Thank you."

She felt his words deep in her heart. "I care about you—and Topher. So, I'm glad to be there for you."

"It means a lot. But no, it's not that. I'm feeling out of my element here. I don't have the years on the road that you do and I want to measure up, prove I have what it takes to do this job."

"Zach," she said, reaching for his forearm, "one or two notes in a six-minute song are *not* a problem. Are you kidding? This is an easy fix, and then we have gold. Well, *I'd* call it gold." She fished, wondering how he felt about their collaboration.

He shifted, reached for her and took her hand in his, squeezed. Electricity passed between them. "I would too. I can't believe how much I love working with you."

"This is the beginning of something, I think, though I don't know what yet," she risked saying. "But first, let's concentrate and replace these measures, okay?" It seemed important to him to redo them rather than have Jon correct them.

"You really don't think I'm the weak link?"

"I believe in you. Completely."

Jon reappeared, and they got back to recording. This time the take worked, and soon they had the raw materials for a finished song. Jon would send it later that day, but Zach and Kate were free to go.

In the parking lot, she offered again, "If you need someone to watch Topher or you boys need a meal or anything, I got you."

"Thanks."

She lifted a prayer as he left, asking God to help in every heavy area of his life.

Eighteen

H ave a seat." Cathy pointed Zach to the chair on the other side of her desk. The clock read 2:29, so Topher was in his classroom on the other end of the school right now. "I'm glad you could come in."

"Thanks for setting up this meeting." Though he'd rather not be rude, Zach didn't have patience for small talk. "What does the psychologist think is happening?"

"First, let me say that Topher hit if off very well with Dr. Jenkins. She has a way with children. If you set up his treatment with her, following our conversation, I believe it will be a fruitful and helpful course."

That brought peace of mind, but Zach needed the diagnosis. He leaned forward. "Did she put a name to what we're dealing with here?"

"SAD. Are you familiar?"

"Well, he certainly has seemed sad." But Zach felt similarly.

"Not sadness, but s-a-d. It stands for Seasonal Affective Disorder, and it refers to the condition of feeling down or even clinically depressed as the days grow shorter this time of year."

That sure clicked. "Would that explain his moodiness and fatigue?" Zach thought for a moment. "He doesn't always even want to eat. But in the spring and summer, he's a different person."

"Yes, all of those symptoms are a confirmation. Dr. Jenkins asked him which season he liked best, how he felt during other months of the year, in addition to other assessment questions."

Finally. Answers. "Is there a medication, or should we move to the tropics or what?" Living this far from the equator, they experienced sunset early but the skies, especially on overcast days, could darken as early as 1:30 and never regain their daytime brightness from November to January. To Zach, fewer daylight hours was a nuisance, but it didn't make him moody.

"There are treatments. Dr. Jenkins recommended scheduling with her office right away, and she wants to meet with you separately. She said there is a way to overcome the symptoms, without moving." Cathy grinned at him.

"So, in yours and her opinions, you both didn't feel this was related to losses?"

"That's definitely a part. But as you've said, he was energetic and cheerful during the warmer, brighter months. That leads us to believe this is based on how much light he experiences and the chemical balances in his brain."

The sun set just after Topher got home from school every day. No wonder he didn't get enough light—he couldn't play outside for long even on cloudy winter days during the week. "Is this kind of thing hereditary?"

"Not necessarily. If you're concerned about your own emotional and mental health, please see a counselor for adults about this. When you take Topher in, you may learn things about yourself and be able to apply what you're learning for his sake. Keep an open mind."

"Definitely. Mental health is just as important as physical health. Topher's mother and I always agreed on that."

"Good." She sighed. "You have no idea how many times I have to defend my field to parents. The same adults who would take their kids to see the bone specialist for a fracture will rule out seeing a psychologist for mental or emotional health. Justifying can get wearying."

"I bet." But Hannah had minored in psychology, so he deeply respected the field. And his therapy after Hannah's death had benefited him. "What are the next steps?"

"Call Dr. Jenkins's office. They'll see you as soon as they can squeeze you in. Topher's out of school for winter break as of December twenty-first, which means he'll be able to focus on feeling better."

"Yeah, usually after the holidays I've noticed he perks back up."

"January has noticeably longer days here, and spring starts in February."

He nodded and stood. "This has been helpful. Thank you for coordinating it."

"Happy to." She stood as well. "Before you leave, I need to get your permission to mention this to his teacher. Would you like to set up a meeting to discuss it with her, or would you mind if I brought her into the loop?"

"Well, since I don't know for sure what's next, I'd like to get more info before I speak to her. But you can tell her that we may be onto something."

"I'll do that. Information like this helps our staff. For example, I had a student break down into tears one December from SAD. The faculty knew about the diagnosis, and we were able to step in with the right approach."

His lungs deflated with a long exhale. A heavy weight still rested on his shoulders. But they could now move forward.

"Treatment is simple at first–Dr. Jenkins will show you. No medications to track. If he responds well, we go from there. If he doesn't respond to any of the treatments, we may find we've got an inaccurate diagnosis. But in my professional opinion, I believe we've landed on the correct answer. Also, Dr. Jenkins is one of the best child psychologists in the area. I've never met someone as thorough. She's helped a lot of our kids in the past. She knows her stuff."

Zach shook Cathy's hand. "Thank you. I'll

keep you updated."

Nineteen

Heath's bombardment of phone calls and texts began around six thirty in the morning. Kate rolled over, wishing she'd remembered to silence her phone the night before.

"Mistletoe" had hit the streaming outlets this week, and Kate hadn't been able to keep up with the buzz. Despite her doubts, mid-December seemed a prime time to release a Christmas composition. She'd tried to get in touch with Zach, but since their studio date, he'd pulled way back. She knew he was busy with his son, so she didn't take it personally. But they'd been building toward something—she thought. Of course her own back-and-forth on whether she was falling for him confused her.

Her phone buzzed with another text from Heath. She didn't need his permission to release a song in her own name, which she'd done—along with Zach's. When she mentioned her plan to the other ensemble members, they'd cheered her on, not at all worried about her commitment to the group. She could hug them for their faith in her. After the release, Nelson and Beth had texted her congratulations. Haley had given her a fist bump for finally stepping out on her own, distancing herself even more from Heath and his controlling ways.

Why was he burning up her phone? Did he want to take credit for the song? Shame her for not saving it for the album? Not that a Christmas song would fit their plan. She didn't bother to read his texts, since she could guess their content after a quick skim. Sitting up, she answered when he called again a few minutes later.

"Hello, Heath." A sense of déjà vu hit her. They'd been here too often. Why couldn't he take no for an answer?

"Tell me what's going on. I thought you were committed to Prism Effect and writing music for our next album. What is this new 'Mistletoe' song I keep hearing about?" He'd never admit he'd listened to it, even if he'd memorized every note.

"I don't owe you any explanations for what I choose to do with my time."

"Yes, you do," he fairly screamed into the phone.

She disconnected, breathing hard. She couldn't remember him using that tone before. If he'd always been this unhinged, there was no way she'd have dated him. Maybe it wasn't that she didn't have the ability to judge character correctly, but rather that Heath had hidden his true self from her. Or she'd fallen for the deception and chosen not to see.

Lord, please help my eyes be open to the truth from here on. Truth sets me free. I don't have to be afraid of it.

Her phone rang again, and she debated blocking him. Instead, she answered, speaking first. "You will not yell at me. One more time and I will hang up, and I will block your number. Do you understand?"

He huffed into the phone like a scolded toddler. "Fine." She heard his clenched teeth in his word. "Can you explain why you've released a song, independently of the group? I thought"—he took a long breath as if trying to calm himself, and she had to hand it to him; he'd kept his tone mostly civil—"you had agreed to write for our next album. Exclusively."

"I did agree to write for our next album. I will keep that agreement." Her words dried up.

"You proceed with this nonsense and I may be forced to make a tough decision."

She didn't respond. His lack of legal grounds hollowed out his threats.

"You're not going to say anything else?"

"Oh, Merry Christmas." She hung up again. Why give him more opportunities to lambaste her for finding her independence? Clearly, when he didn't get his way, the man lost his mind. *Thank You, Lord, that I did not end up married to him.*

She checked her sources again and noted the growing sales numbers. She needed to get ahold of Zach, if he answered this time, and share the good news.

"Five more minutes, Toph." Zach squinted

toward the therapy light box where his son sat. "Keep your eyes closed."

The therapist had said that children were too tempted to look directly at the light bulbs and that that could be detrimental, so if they prescribed phototherapy for them, they warned them not to stare directly into the unit. But asking a boy Topher's age to sit still, face close to the light, eyes shut for part of the session, and listen to the ticking clock was like asking them to pull the moon down and hold it on their laps. Crazy.

But the non-drug therapy helped. Apparently, Topher *needed* sunlight. His therapist had met with him three times since that meeting in Cathy's office. She'd discussed Hannah's death and agreed with Zach that the kiddo was of course still grieving, but he wasn't stuck. He'd experienced normal progression in his grief, nothing to concern them, and it certainly didn't explain his extreme moodiness. So, they'd continued to rule out other factors—asking about possible bullies or school worries. Nothing made sense, except SAD.

Zach wouldn't have believed the positive effect that light therapy could have until he'd seen it himself. The process was like taking Topher to Hawaii, or Florida, playing outside in the sunlight, bringing him back, and then getting on with his daily life. He perked up. If he was sleepy, it woke him up. His mood swings stabilized, all without medicine. Trouble lifted from his little shoulders. Though they conducted these therapy sessions in the morning, Topher didn't seem as anxious in the evenings.

Thank You, Lord, for breakthroughs. The burden of Topher's suffering had weighed Zach down more than he'd known and now that his kiddo was doing a bit better, Zach could breathe again. Hopefully, his own diagnosis would be as easy to address. He'd set all that aside in the last weeks.

Lay down the burden.

Lord, thank You for that invitation. Help me to trust that You see, You know, and You've got this. Please carry every burden for me: Toph's condition, health, finances, the future. My feelings about Kate.

Those still confused him, but he couldn't see clear answers, especially with his son's new therapist now giving him advice.

Zach's phone buzzed on the kitchen

counter, and he saw Kate's name. "Hey," he answered. "Sorry I've been out of it. Things are a bit overwhelming here." Maybe one day he would overcome his tendency to avoid tough situations when he felt overwhelmed.

"Hi. Thanks for taking my call. Can we talk for a minute? I have good news."

"Sure." Zach kept an eye on Topher. "Two more minutes, buddy," he said to him. "Okay, Kate, I'm all yours." He wished. Though he tried to deny it, he was still drawn to her. What would happen when she learned about his decision?

"Um"—her voice cracked as if the wording of his automatic response meant something to her too—"I wanted to let you know 'Mistletoe' is selling really well. We're climbing the rankings in several places online. Early reviewers are gushing."

"Sweet." He'd hoped for success—for her sake. It had been a fun fantasy to write together. Of course, now he needed to get back to his normal life.

He'd picked up his worries again. *Sorry, Lord. I know You've got me.*

Topher darted off the barstool when the light box switched off. "Woohoo!"

Zach grinned and refocused on his call. "Distracted over here. Go ahead, Kate. I'm back."

"No problem." She gave him a moment. "I don't know if it's clicking for you yet. Sales like these equal *cha-ching.* We deduct for Jon and the studio time, and the rest is ours. I'll have a big check for you soon."

"What?" Zach stared unseeing toward the counter. He hadn't expected to do more than help her out, and certainly not to receive much as repayment. The news he had for Kate wasn't nearly as cheerful as what she alluded to.

"That's how this works. And it's only the beginning. We'll probably sell downloads into January as people tell their friends and family about it."

"Wow." Of course "big check" could mean anything, so Zach reined in his hopes. Then, he cringed. How did God feel about Zach withholding hope? If Topher came to Zach with his Christmas wish list and Zach had the resources, Zach would *hope* that Topher wouldn't walk away despondent about getting any of his favorite presents. Was that what Zach's doubt did to God? *I'm trying here, Lord.*

Please help. The way God kept interrupting his thoughts, challenging him, comforted Zach today. Those interactions proved God's personal involvement.

"I have a proposal for you. When can we get together?"

What did she have in mind? "Want to meet at the church? Tonight could work, if that's not too short of notice."

"Yes. How about six? This could be good news for us."

Given her enthusiasm, he hated to bring his own update. "See you then."

He helped Topher finish getting ready for school. Zach hadn't had the courage to bring up what the counselor had advised regarding his son. And days ago when Dr. Jenkins suggested it, Zach hadn't wanted to follow her latest advice. But for Topher, he would, even though it seemed counterintuitive.

He just didn't relish telling Kate. Or saying goodbye.

Twenty

Kate stepped into King Church's large building where she'd attended since relocating to Whidbey. Colorful Christmas swags hung over doorways, and a huge tree, decorated with oversized ornaments, occupied a corner of the lobby.

Zach approached from the hallway leading away from the sanctuary. "Hey, Kate." She imagined him walking right up to her for a hug, but he kept his distance.

"Is Topher here?"

Zach pocketed his hands. "He's with my sister and his cousins." He seemed anxious tonight. Why? Had he learned bad news from his doctor?

"I miss him," she said aloud before she

could stop herself. Silly, though, because they would see each other a lot more if her proposal worked for Zach. Plus, it'd only been a little over a week since they'd hung out together. "I know I just saw you both," she admitted, feeling chagrin sweep over her. But Zach's face showed he might not agree. Had she been missed too? "Everything okay?" she asked as apprehension stirred in her stomach.

"Since the building isn't technically open, I don't want to leave this unlocked." He strode to the front doors and secured them. "Let's chat over there." He pointed at a lounge area.

"Sure thing." She waited for him, and then they walked together toward the tree and seating area.

Zach sat in an overstuffed chair, adjacent to the couch, and Kate settled on the end of the sofa. The man sure kept his distance. She'd have agreed with that choice before. Now, she'd changed her mind. But would he? She decided to be direct. "Are you sure everything's all right? You seem worried about something." She wanted to hear him out first. Then, her good news might cheer him up.

"I need to update you on Topher."

She set her purse aside and shrugged out of

her coat. Shifting to the edge of her seat, she said, "Yes, please."

"His counselor diagnosed him, and we've started treatment." Zach leaned back, crossing one ankle over his thigh, but then, he shifted as if uncomfortable.

"That's good. I'm so glad you have answers. Is it serious?"

"It's treatable, and he's already responding well." Gripping the chair's arms, Zach planted both feet on the floor like he was gearing up for something.

"Whew. I'm sure that's a load off your mind." She reached for his forearm, but he pulled back. "Has something else happened?"

"I'll tell you in just a minute. First, update me on our song."

She liked hearing him call it theirs. Her heart filled up. "Well, it's trending hot right now and I have a check for you." Normally, they wouldn't be paid yet, but she'd pay herself back later. Her savings could withstand this, and the sales would cover it. She reached into her bag and pulled out the cashier's check she'd drafted at the bank. Before she handed it to him, though, she needed to know something. "Is your pastor angry about you doing this side project?"

His face turned earnest. "No. And I don't regret it either. At all." His expression warmed, and she drank it in.

"I'm relieved. Because I wouldn't want you to get in trouble." She'd faced enough persecution from Heath for their endeavor without learning it had caused Zach grief too. Every text from Heath lately hinted at revenge.

"How did Prism Effect react? I mean, did they know you were going rogue for the season?" He allowed himself a grin, and it undid a new corner of her heart.

"Heath hates it. But whatevs, right? Beth, Nelson, and Haley are all behind us."

His expression softened even further. "Good."

She handed him the check and watched his face.

He peeked at it, then did a double take. "Whoa. That is a lot of digits."

She chuckled. She'd often held checks with that many digits. It was fun to see the experience through his eyes.

"We must have sold thousands of copies."

"Tens of thousands, and the number is climbing. It's a niche fan base, but once they get wind of a new piece, they share it like crazy. Everyone loves our Christmas duet."

His eyes rounded. "It's only been a few days."

She shrugged. "I think people figured out the tie to Prism Effect, even though we didn't include that name. So," she said, scooting forward again. "I have a proposal for you."

He still seemed in shock, but he pocketed the folded check and met her eyes. "Shoot." Something delicious about the way he zeroed in on her, as if romance hovered beneath the surface with their words hinting at their chemistry. Or maybe he didn't hear her expression the same way she did, not that she'd meant to *propose*.

Focus.

"With this positive feedback, and I know we agreed to cowrite for the next Prism Effect album—I hope you're still on board for that—" Her words gushed out. She'd written several pieces already in the last few days. Finally. *Thanks, Lord.*

He reached for her, took her hand, and she held her breath. He hadn't touched her tonight until now. "Easy, Kate. Breathe."

Her nerves calmed with his hand gripping

hers. She let herself relax.

"Better?"

"Much." Maybe they were okay after all. Having Heath dump her unexpectedly had thrown her. Crazy she could still worry about being cut out of someone's life without notice, even now. Heath's actions might haunt her for a while. But she'd made a decision. She'd no longer rule out dating a pianist. Not with Zach sitting there, smelling like Christmas and smiling so kindly at her. Sure, she didn't know him like she would once they'd gotten even better acquainted, but she trusted him. He wouldn't cut off ties from out of nowhere. She'd asked God to open her eyes and not let her miss obvious warnings, like she'd done with Heath. As Zach's hazel eyes gazed into hers, she liked what she saw.

Courage rushed through her veins. "So, how would you feel about cowriting and recording a whole album full of Christmas songs, for release next year, of course, and we'd include 'Mistletoe' on the album, perhaps as the title song." She kept her words slower this time. What had she been worried about? This was Zach. They had a rapport. They had chemistry. They made beautiful music toge—

He tugged his hand away. "I can't."

"But you've seen the positive response."

"Maybe come spring, but right now I can't commit to anything further."

"Wait." Her pulse shot up. "What happened?" It felt like Zach had gotten what he wanted—a paycheck—and he was done with her, except for their upcoming performance at this church. That wasn't like him. That was *Heath*, not Zach. *Please don't be like Heath.* He'd just held her hand. He couldn't simply move on—either professionally or romantically, could he? "Was this just an experiment?" she asked him. And even if it was, why not try for more success? Not that she preferred he want her solely for her music or her name or her fame.

Had he used her?

She sat back, waiting, studying him.

"Of course not." He ran his tongue over his lower teeth. "I hate this . . ." He sighed and then seemed to decide he had to follow through with whatever was on his mind. "For Topher," he murmured. Then, he faced her again. "My son's therapist had advice for us about Topher's stability."

"Okay . . ."

"She wants us to keep things simple. Just school and the holidays and church. Nothing extra. No big changes."

What wasn't he saying? "Does she know how Topher brightened up whenever he visited? He needs kind friends right now. Maybe if you explained . . ."

"I did." Zach grimaced as if the situation pained him too. "She specifically mentioned not adding new relationships, and of course, not moving away or changing schools or anything else upsetting."

"Upsetting?" How had Haley and Kate been upsetting?

Except Topher had acted out during one of their get-togethers. But his recent enjoyment seemed to overshadow his angst.

"As his father, can't you override advice, even professional counsel, if you know more details? I mean, you know how much Christmas means to him and spending the season together has been amazing." Her throat burned. "For all of us. I thought."

He groaned, standing. "For now, I think we need to do what the counselor says. Her treatment is working." Was he simply putting on a brave I'll-sacrifice-anything-for-my-son face, or was he that indifferent about her? Not that she'd make him choose. She'd just guessed wrong. Like with Heath.

"I'm sorry," he said again, his shoulders rounded. "Topher means everything to me, especially after losing his mother." His soft voice cracked. "I can't take any chances with him slipping into a deep depression."

She didn't want that either. How isolating themselves over Christmas could possibly be good for either of them baffled her. But it was obvious she wouldn't change his mind. "Do you still want me to play at the program on Christmas Eve?"

"Please."

She'd put on her professional persona and power through. What choice was there?

He walked her to the door, waited for her to pull out her car keys. She stood there, shaking her head, truly not comprehending what had just happened. She'd come tonight, full of hope, and been shot down. And obviously she had misread him. If they'd been about to begin a romantic relationship, wouldn't Zach want to lean on her? Like that day at the studio when he'd needed to meet with the counselor?

She wanted him to trust her and rely on her. And she'd imagined leaning on him, commiserating about Heath's obnoxious backlash.

Clearly, she'd been alone in this almost-relationship.

She reached to push against the crash bar, but he stretched around her. She felt his breath against her ear. "I'm so sorry," he repeated, whispering. She wanted to close her eyes and drink in the scent, his nearness.

But she forced herself to pass him. "I'll be in touch with further royalties if you wanna text me your mailing address. Goodbye."

She wanted him to reach for her arm, tug her back, say he didn't mean to shut her out. But he was silent as he closed the door. She made her way to her car with a heavy heart.

Only extreme willpower kept Zach from following Kate. That look in her eyes, how crestfallen she'd seemed. Now his chest ached. He'd done the best thing, right? Topher needed stability. Kate had once mentioned moving down to Gig Harbor. This decision was better in the long run, even if she would be on island through Christmas.

He went through the motions of shutting down lights. The still, dimly lit sanctuary beckoned him. The check crinkled in his pocket when he crossed his arms. This would cover his bills. Easily. And he'd be able to buy gifts for Topher. They'd be okay. If the song kept selling through December at the same rate, he'd probably receive another hefty sum from Kate. He'd wanted to keep his commitment to cowrite with her for January, and he liked the idea of releasing a Christmas album with her next year. But she'd probably change her mind now.

Maybe he should call her. But he couldn't abandon his son this time of year. And in order to get a lot of work done in the next couple of weeks, Kate and Zach would need to spend hours and hours together, without Topher. He couldn't see a way around this choice between Topher and Kate.

He drove to his sister's place and found his son asleep on the couch. Even on light therapy treatment, he still got tired within three hours after sunset on most nights.

"Dad?" Topher asked as Zach woke him up. "Where's Miss Kate? I wanna see her and Miss

Haley."

Lacy nodded toward Topher. "He wouldn't stop talking about them. He kept saying how much it would cheer him up to hang out with them. That they made Christmastime feel happy." Lacy leaned close to whisper in Zach's ear while he held Topher in his arms. "He cried for about an hour over it."

Zach's heart dropped. "He did?" That was something, in all these dark weeks, that Topher rarely did. Was he descending into a new level toward depression? The therapist wanted stability, but what if Kate's kindness provided that?

"Yeah, so don't make any hasty decisions. I mean, I get it that your . . . advisors mentioned that course of action," she said, using vague language in front of Topher. "But c'mon, even I can see how good they are for both of you."

Zach could see it too. Kate had questioned whether Zach shouldn't override the counselor's advice. Lacy agreed, it seemed. And Topher spending the evening crying, thinking he was missing out on Kate time? Yeah, Zach could cry to.

He needed to make this right.

Twenty-One

Once again, Heath wouldn't take no for an answer. After a week of threatening texts and attempted calls, he'd repeatedly called this morning. She silenced her phone for a quiet breakfast. Low fog hovered over the bay as the day brightened with sunrise. One month had changed everything. She'd come up here in mid-November, met Zach, overcome writer's block, fallen for Topher and his dad. If Haley could hear her thoughts, she'd laugh outright. Okay, Kate could at least admit it to herself.

She'd fallen for Zach.

Not that her feelings mattered. He'd given up on the two of them. The last few days since he'd shared his decision had slipped by in a blur. She'd buried herself in composing and come up with a new piece every day. They needed polishing, but Prism Effect could re-work what she had and plan which ones to record.

Her phone's screen lit up again. What? Was Heath dying? Such a drama queen. She rolled her eyes and flipped her phone over. She'd get to him. After enjoying her hot cocoa.

Pulling a notebook closer, she made a list of the worries she currently carried. Starting with Zach, Topher, Prism Effect, touring, the new album, housing. All of those burdens felt heavy. She couldn't solve any of the puzzles, except interim housing. Come January, Kate would move into Beth's second bedroom since her roommate had just moved to Europe.

"Carol of the Bells" played softly from her MP3 player, and a verse came to mind. *Give all your worries and cares to God, for he cares about you.* She'd try it. Somewhere, she'd heard about praying while picturing burdens as physical objects and either handing them directly to Jesus or laying them at His feet.

Finished with her drink, she grabbed her notebook and headed for the living area where she sat in a chair, facing the bay. Wrapped in a chunky knit blanket, she prayed through her list. *Lord, I need Your help. I don't have the solutions. But You do. Please work all of this out. And if it's possible, please help us find a way to...* What? What did she want?

She wanted Zach and Topher in her life. She wanted... Well, she wanted what Topher wanted—for them to be a family.

What about her touring schedule and Topher's need for stability? What about Zach's decision to shut her out of their lives? So many unknowns, obstacles to them being together.

Nothing is impossible for Me.

True. So true. A wave of peace covered her. God's nearness was all she needed. She'd focus on what was in front of her, keep her commitments, and pray through all that lay ahead.

This time when Heath called, she answered. "Hello, Heath. What's going on?" She tried to keep any irritation out of her voice while she dreaded his probable threats.

"I still can't believe you'd betray us like that. I thought you were committed to the group."

She wouldn't dignify his accusations with a response. Instead she waited, reminding herself his words were untrue. *She'd* founded

Prism Effect, served as the main composer for the ensemble, invested time, money, and sweat into making the group a success. For years.

Obviously, he hadn't found a legal recourse. If he had, he'd have led with that—how he was going to sue her or some such. But she'd checked and she was within her rights to record whatever she wanted, wherever she wanted, and with whomever she wanted. Heath hated being left out of a successful turn.

When she didn't react, he huffed into the phone. "So, since you gave up on us, I'm giving up on Prism Effect. I quit."

Huh. Well, that would solve one problem. She barely withheld a guffaw into his ear. *Wow, Lord, You work fast sometimes.*

"Did you hear me?"

"Yes, I did." She pressed her lips together.

"That means I will no longer be writing, recording, playing, or touring with the group."

"Have you notified the others?" She needed his words at least witnessed by Beth or Nelson, or both. "Could you send us all an e-mail to that effect?"

"Check your inbox."

"Okay, then, I wish you the best with

everything." She clicked off the phone call and let out a cheer. Then, she blocked his number. No more harassment from him.

She spent the next forty-five minutes in a video call with Nelson and Beth. After they all celebrated Heath's leaving, they discussed next steps. All three had received the e-mail, which Beth promised to print out and keep handy as proof. It'd be just like Heath to crash their recording sessions, so Nelson promised to notify their producer, Jon, as well.

Now they needed a pianist. "I have the perfect person in mind," Kate offered. "If you want, I could get in touch with him and let you both know how that goes. He's excellent."

"Is he the one you recorded 'Mistletoe' with?" Of course, Beth would have deduced the connection. "Because that guy is off-the-charts good."

"Yes, he is." And wouldn't Zach love hearing that? He'd battled insecurity during the studio session, but Beth picked up on his genius just as Kate had.

"And you're buddies with him?" Nelson asked.

"Or more," Beth singsonged.

"I wish," Kate murmured. "I gotta go, peeps.

We'll talk soon."

They all clicked off, and Kate pondered how and when to bring up her invitation. Would Zach even consider joining Prism Effect? And how would that influence Topher's health?

More burdens to pray about. But one thing she knew for sure was that Zach was the best choice for their group, and a strong sense of rightness hit her whenever she considered that choice.

Now, she needed a chance to ask him.

Twenty-Two

Zach met Clay Garrison, Liberty Winfield, Jaelyn Neill and her parents, Nick and Amanda, at the church's front doors. "Welcome and Merry Christmas!" He donned his professional persona. Already Topher had begun to slip into increasing sadness since Zach told him Miss Kate and Miss Haley weren't going to spend Christmas with them. Zach and Kate would perform with Topher tonight. Then, Zach needed to talk to her and fix his mistake.

"The kids are meeting back in the chapel, Jaelyn, if you want to head in."

"Merry Christmas," Clay said, holding Liberty's hand. "Thanks for putting this together tonight."

"Yeah," Nick said, arm around his wife, Amanda. "Jaelyn can't wait to perform with the bell choir."

"I heard them rehearsing earlier this week," Liberty said. "They sound great."

The four of them excused themselves to find seats and Zach greeted a few more families, directing kiddos to the chapel and inviting parents to take programs and find seating. Since the word had gotten out that he and Kate from Prism Effect were going to play their duet, they'd expected a larger than usual crowd. Already seating filled up. They'd make use of the foyer if needed, or perhaps Zach and Kate would perform an encore at the midnight service.

Lacy and Adam had arrived earlier, taking Topher and his cousins to the chapel. Topher seemed okay, even happy that they'd get to play together. He'd done well during their practice sessions this month, while Kate and Zach had successfully pulled off professional distance. He cringed.

He only hoped Kate would listen to him if he got a chance to talk with her alone.

Why hadn't Zach prayed about his decision before pushing Kate away? Because though he was learning to take his burdens to God, he still wasn't very practiced—apparently—at praying before acting. Of course, Zach still couldn't solve the logistical problems. Kate belonged on the road, touring. Topher needed stability. But Zach would trust his instincts and what God had revealed to him.

Kate appeared in the foyer, toting her instrument, wearing a burgundy velvet dress. His breath evaporated. "I need to talk to you after this," she said quietly, once she'd gotten close enough.

He smiled. "Me too and this time it's good news."

Relief seemed to pour from her. "Mine too."

The program went along smoothly with the bell choir starting things off to rousing applause. The children's songs followed, bringing parents to tears. Topher seemed comfortable singing with the choir. Then, it was time for Kate's performances. They began with 'Carol of the Bells' with Topher. He held the gleaming bell still until needed, obeying all the directives Zach had given him for controlling the sound. He did a remarkable job, and the audience loved the trio. When they finished, Topher set his bell down and darted over to Kate, whom he hugged. Zach felt a catch in his throat. Poor kid. He was probably more confused than he would have been had Zach not put them all on a roller coaster of conflicted choices.

Kate fairly glowed as Topher scampered off to run backstage.

At the mic, Zach spoke. "Tonight, we have a special performance for you, our church family and friends. As many of you know, this is Kate Fleming of the popular ensemble Prism Effect." Zach waited for the applause to fade. "She's visiting for the holidays, and we've cowritten a song. We're thrilled," he said, looking at her, "that she's here. Without further ado, this is our Christmas duet entitled 'Mistletoe.'" Teens in the front row *oohed*, and Zach grinned. Well, so be it.

Performing with Kate made Zach feel like they'd stepped back into the mansion and sat alone, music rising to the cathedral ceilings. Oh, he wanted more of this. Of course, he couldn't leave his job as music director here. "Mistletoe" would probably only sell well through the first part of January, and then Zach would go back to obscurity.

But he would tell Kate how he felt and give

her the option of whether she wanted to be a part of their lives somehow.

Following their performance, thunderous applause filled the packed auditorium. Kate set her cello in its stand and joined Zach for a bow. He pulled her close to his side, and she wrapped an arm behind him.

Backstage, two hours later, Zach took both of her hands. Topher had gone home with Lacy while Zach finished his church duties following the family service. No one else milled around in this quiet classroom. "Mind playing that one more time for the midnight service?"

"Not at all." Her eyes sparkled with joy. Was that just holiday happiness or something else?

"First, I need to say that I'm an idiot."

She pressed her lips tightly together, laughter in her expression.

"Of course I can decide if something is beneficial to my son. And you, Kate Fleming with your beautiful cello playing and kindness, are beneficial to my son."

"Am I?"

"Well, he hasn't cried anymore when we play together." Zach still didn't understand all Topher's moods or reasons. But he had hope, and his son fared better surrounded by people who cared for him. People like Kate and Haley.

"Am I only beneficial to Topher?"

He tugged her closer. "And maybe his dad too. See? I'm not afraid to say it."

"I have a feeling you're arguing with someone who isn't here right now."

"Guilty."

"Well, I have news too. Heath's out."

"He is?"

"Apparently, I 'betrayed the group' and he can't live with that—or he was jealous—so he resigned."

Zach shook his head, unable to imagine the foolishness. Wouldn't Kate's new song's popularity bring more name recognition, and sales, to Prism Effect's next album?

"His loss may be our gain," Kate said.

"What do you mean?"

"Beth and Nelson love your work on our duet. And we need a pianist. All three of us want you to seriously consider joining Prism Effect."

He blinked, taken aback. "What?"

"I know it's complicated with Topher and traveling and all that... Honestly, I have no idea how it would work, but I want us to brainstorm ways we *could* make it work because the group needs you. *I* need you. I've fallen for you, Zach Tillmon."

Her words felt like music. "You have?"

"Mm-hmm. See? I wasn't afraid to say it." She grinned at her repeated words.

"What about your rule to never date your piano player again?"

"Well," she said, shrugging, "that may have been idiotic too."

"I want to keep making music with you."

She nodded, smiling. "Same."

"When do we have to decide?"

"We're due in studio next month, so New Year's?"

Having that income, touring as a musician, Zach couldn't picture a better future. And joining his favorite ensemble? That had dreams-come-true winding through it. But what did Topher need?

"I should mention that my medical appointments resume in January too." Scared him a little, but having her support would help so much.

"I'd be glad to help however I can." She squeezed his hands. "I don't have the answers, even now. But I don't want to stop what God starts."

"Me either." He leaned down and kissed her, softly. She answered with a kiss that helped silence his doubts. He pulled her closer, taking his time and savoring every second.

When he finally pulled away, he rested his forehead against hers. They didn't have everything worked out for their futures, but God would show them if they asked. And for now, that was enough. "My son really wants to see you and Miss Haley tomorrow. Can you come over? Or can we come to you?"

"We'll see you at the mansion."

"He's going to be so happy. And so is his dad."

"Merry Christmas," she said, tugging him back toward her.

"Merry Christmas," he said before kissing her again.

A Note from the Author

I was glad to revisit Whidbey Island as the third book in my Washington Island Romance Series is set there. I took artistic license with my location names as I'm loosely basing my town on an actual city.

I also took some license with how quickly a musical artist could get a song out to the marketplace and how quickly sales statistics would be reported.

You may have noticed that my musical ensemble's name and the publishing company name match in this novella. That's purposeful as I created them. Look for more books from Prism Effect Publishing in the future.

As with the stories in my novel trilogy, I included a psychological aspect. I used a known diagnosis, but in order to fit my purposes in this novella, I took some license with the treatment.

Music is such a central part of the Christmas season. Our family especially enjoys instrumental carols, including some arrangements with piano and cello. Pairing professional musicians in this novella allowed me to include that fun aspect. Look for mention of these characters' music in future Washington Island Christmas novellas!

Burdens can weigh us down, can't they? It is my prayer that you'll have Jesus's peace this season. I know God is able and willing to carry our burdens if we drop them at His feet. (1 Peter 5:7)

I hope you enjoy this taste of Christmas on Puget Sound.

Merry Christmas!

All His best,

Annette

Acknowledgments

Sincere gratitude goes to Todd Gowers, adjunct professor of music, Seattle Pacific University, who answered my questions regarding my heroine's cello playing and professional life. Any mistakes are mine.

I'm grateful to Dawn Kinzer for her steadfast and enjoyable company on this writing journey. She and I go way back as critique partners. I loved working with her on the original collection where her and my novellas both appeared. You are a gift, my dear friend.

Hugs and thanks to the rest of my McCritters, Ocieanna Fleiss and Veronica McCann. I still draw on what we learned together while munching on fries and closing those places down. Miss our get-togethers.

Much love, as always, to my supportive family. Thank you for cheering me on and praying for me as I work on these fiction projects!

Thank you to the libraries that carry my books and the bookstores and dear readers who order them. May you have hours of enjoyment in the pleasure of reading.

My dad enjoys words and always set an example of enjoying vocabulary and the love of learning. His is a standard for a strong work ethic and entrepreneurship, launching his own successful home businesses during my childhood. I'm grateful for that model. I love you, Dad.

My precious mother displayed a pattern of voracious reading for me while I grew up. I recall visits to the quiet, small-town library where she would later serve for over twenty years. Now, my books sit on those shelves. My siblings and I enjoyed hearing her read Bible stories at bedtime. I'm forever grateful to her for her example of unwavering faith and the love of books. I love you and miss you, Mom. But one day, we will be reunited on streets of gold. I'll meet you at the gate.

Biggest thanks to Jesus, the Author and Finisher of my faith, for Your presence and this calling, and for hope. All my love.

About the Author

Award-winning author **Annette M. Irby** loves reading and has enjoyed writing since her teen years. Her novel, *Finding Love on Bainbridge Island, Washington*, won the Selah Award in 2019. Her novel *Finding Love on Whidbey Island, Washington,* finaled in the 2020 Cascade Award contest. She is a freelance editor at AMI Editing. Married over thirty years, she and her husband enjoy spending time with their family at the beach.

Learn more at her website: AnnetteMIrby.com

Connect with Annette on Facebook by joining her readers group at this web address: www.facebook.com/groups/annettemirbyreaderfriends

Find Annette's other books at her Amazon author page at the following web address: Amazon.com/author/annette_m_irby.com

For book club questions, please visit the Books page tab on Annette's website.

A Christmas Romance

Washington Island Christmas
Book Two

Chapter One

Don't let him get to you.

A muscle pulled tight in Eli Jaxon's back as he set his end of the heavy foam mattress onto the base. He stood, stretching. He'd known his brother, Tyler, would antagonize him. The whole family made allowances for Ty right now. By age forty, he shouldn't need them. Except what did Eli know? Eight years older, Ty was more second father than brother sometimes. Lately? Civility barked unheeded orders from the sidelines. Heh. If Eli wrote adult fiction, he'd tap the phrase into his phone. But *his* readership wouldn't grasp those vocab words.

"C'mon, Eustace." As if he had something to prove, Ty was already at the doorway of the townhome's main bedroom, ready to run another load. "We're doing this for you, the least you can do is keep up."

Let it go. Eli ground his teeth, ignoring the name his brother used. He followed Ty's scuffing soles down the wood stairs.

Dad grunted as he shoved one end of the sofa into place against the great room's longest wall. "This place probably isn't what you're accustomed to in NYC." As if sensing tension between the brothers, Dad seasoned his words with compassion and understanding.

Eli glanced around his new place here on Bainbridge Island, Washington. The housing complex was only a few years old, and his unit contained the usual elements—open plan, black granite, wood flooring, gray walls, big picture windows. Why a designer would choose gray for interior colors in the Pacific Northwest Eli couldn't guess. Popularity? And not letting in the fresh air? Frustrating. Eh, it would do.

Since when did he care about fancy or luxurious though? No need to flaunt your money when simple sufficed. Sure, he'd once enjoyed an apartment in New York. But he'd worked hard to afford it, and there was no shame in that. Not after what he'd come back from.

"Definitely not a penthouse." Ty reappeared at the front door with a nightstand in hand. Cold, wet wind rushed in around him to fill the room with whiffs of pine and snow, though it only rained locally. Peaks of the nearby Cascade and Olympic Ranges horded all flakes so far this month, layering up for ski season. While powder fell by the foot, covering the mountains, winds scented the area with snow region wide.

"Cool it, Ty," Dad scolded. Eli held his tongue. He'd heard that tone enough times. Even Ty flinched, a tic in his jaw.

Mom joined them from the hall bath. Her short, white-blond highlighted hair lay askew, no doubt due to the windy morning. "He's here for *you*, you know."

Ty grunted as he climbed the stairs two at a time, heedless of his bulky load. Suspicion confirmed. Tyler was clearly out to prove something. But what?

Flashbacks of his torn-up older brother gritting his teeth a few years ago following those earlier results punched Eli's memory. *That* was the true Tyler. Not this jerk.

Both Dad and Mom turned apologetic faces toward Eli. "He's just hurting," their father offered.

Mom added, "And scared."

Softening his expression, Eli waved them off. "I get it." Having spent the last few years living across the country, Eli'd avoided most of Ty's moods. Now he was here, whether Ty liked it or not. Even if he shoved him away, like those games as children. Ty challenging his baby brother to wrestling matches to get him to fight back and overpower someone three times bigger.

See if Ty could get Eli to unlock his hold now.

Eli's niece, Cadence, materialized from the den. She seemed regal, for an eleven-year-old. Somewhat wiser since her experience. Eyeing her father as he returned, she said, "Dad, be nice to my uncle. We may need him for a favor one day, you know."

Reaching the bottom step, Ty scoffed. Then, he seemed to shake off his irritation. "Are you feeling okay?" he asked her, and miraculously there was a tenderness in his voice, eyes, and posture.

Eli tried to hide a grimace, but he worried too. They all did.

Cadence rolled her eyes. "I feel fine."

Eli's stomach rumbled. They were probably hungry too. Time to order a sandwich delivery and feed the troops. "Thanks again for helping, everyone." He pulled out his phone. "Lunch in half an hour."

Cady cheered, and Ty headed outside. If his wife were here, he'd probably be less of a bear. But she'd picked up extra shifts at work, trying to help them pay for whatever they might face in the weeks and months ahead. Dad strode out the door to join Ty, maybe knock him around a minute.

"Call me when the food gets here!" Cadence darted upstairs, carefree again.

Eli focused on positioning the area rug under the sofa's front feet.

"I'm so glad you're back, Eli," Mom said, piling a stack of hand towels on the kitchen granite from an open box. "You need to check out the local bookshop in town. You might remember it. We visited when you were a kid."

She couldn't know he usually avoided bookstores these days. They reminded him that people wanted something from him. Finished in the living area, he joined her in the kitchen to stack flatware in the drawer's sorter. He gave her a noncommittal nod.

"Thanks for putting up with your brother."

One glance toward the door verified Ty hadn't returned. "I know he's worried." Eli gripped the counter behind him, locking his elbows, raising his shoulders, vision blurring. If anything happened to Cadence... No. He couldn't go there.

"And he may not understand yet, but your plan is—" A hitch in her voice cut off Mom's words. She shook out a towel and folded it precisely. Eli waited her out. "Well," she began again, "it's extremely generous. Selfless. I mean this place is nice. It's newer and just right for one or two people. But, hon, you could have afforded waterfront. All-cash. A to-die-for view. Whales and sea lions as neighbors."

He scoffed softly and gave her a gentle smile. "I don't need that."

"Like I said. Selfless." She wrapped her arms around him. Though he'd outgrown her in high school, there was nothing like hugging his mother. He rested his face against the top of her head, feeling the kind of comfort that only came from her. "You could have waited to see how things played out. Found a rental here. You know, kept your New York apartment."

"Nah, it's too many unknowns. Plus, I missed you guys."

"Well, I know you gave up a lot. Your father and I are so proud of you," she repeated. "Now, my Christmas prayer is for peace. Between you brothers. In our family. In our hearts."

Yes, Lord.

He tightened his arms around her, inhaling her lilac fragrance. Whether Tyler welcomed him or not, Eli would be here for the journey ahead, for all the unknowns. Sure enough, Ty didn't want him. But he needed him. Just like last time.

Only this time, Eli was here.

To read more of **A Christmas Romance**, find the book on Amazon.com.

www.ingramcontent.com/pod-product-compliance
Lightning Source LLC
Chambersburg PA
CBHW020148310726
48970CB00006B/2058